"I proposed

Evie pulled the blanket up a little bit closer around her and gave a small nod. "That you did."

"Those were the days, huh?" He hadn't meant for his voice to turn quite so soft or quite so wistful, but there it was.

"I felt like such an outsider."

It might've been the last thing he expected her to say. How could she have felt like an outsider? Such a close-knit community, loving family, meddlesome church district. Yet her chin had taken on a sad curve, and her lips pressed together.

He looked at her for as long as he dared, then glanced back at the road. "What about now?"

"Nee." But she hesitated too long before she said the word, and he knew she wasn't telling the complete truth. It wasn't like Evie to lie.

She felt like an outsider? The thought broke his heart.

"Sometimes."

He knew she was just downplaying her troubles. She was the kindest person he knew, and she deserved everything in the world...

Born and bred in Mississippi, **Amy Lillard** is a transplanted Southern belle who now lives in Oklahoma with her deputy husband and two spoiled cats. When she's not creating happy endings, she's an avid football fan (go Chiefs!) and an adoring mother to an almost-adult son and loves binge-watching television shows. Amy is an award-winning author with more than sixty novels and novellas in print. She loves to hear from readers. You can find her on Facebook, Instagram, X, Goodreads, TikTok and Pinterest. You can email her at amylillard@hotmail.com or check out her website, amywritesromance.com.

Books by Amy Lillard

Love Inspired

The Amish Christmas Promise
The Amish Bachelor's Promise

Visit the Author Profile page at LoveInspired.com.

THE AMISH BACHELOR'S PROMISE

AMY LILLARD

LOVE INSPIRED
INSPIRATIONAL ROMANCE

LOVE INSPIRED®
INSPIRATIONAL ROMANCE

ISBN-13: 978-1-335-93194-8

The Amish Bachelor's Promise

Recycling programs for this product may not exist in your area.

Love Inspired
22 Adelaide St. West, 41st Floor
Toronto, Ontario M5H 4E3, Canada
www.LoveInspired.com

Printed in Lithuania

MIX
Paper | Supporting responsible forestry
FSC® C021394

She will do him good and not evil
all the days of her life.
—*Proverbs* 31:12

To everyone who has tried and failed,
always try again.

Chapter One

Everyone was speculating, whispering behind their hands, talking about it as Evie Ebersol poured another cup of water to serve at the after-church meal. People were trying to be discreet. No one wanted to say anything too loudly, but everyone was thinking it.

Poor Freeman Yoder.

As they had gathered that morning for their worship service, it hadn't taken long for one person or maybe even two to notice that Helen Schrock wasn't there. No one in her family had mentioned anything about her being too ill to attend, so all who noticed had started doing the math, adding two and two together to get a whopping four.

During the three hours of their regular worship service, Evie had shifted uncomfortably, knowing for certain what the others, those outside of Helen's family, had only suspected.

Now that church was officially let out, the talk had begun.

"Is it true?" Hedya Peachy asked, her blue eyes flashing from side to side as if to see if anyone else was listening in.

Was it true? Was Helen really gone? That was what she was asking.

Ever since Helen Schrock had broken up with her long-standing boyfriend, Freeman Yoder, she had been talking about going to Lancaster to visit some distant cousin or another and get a feel for how the Amish lived down there. Evie wasn't sure what had gotten into her friend. Helen had always been so peaceful, so stable, so serene. Now all of a sudden she wanted to live a different life than what they had here in the valley.

"She'll be back," a sweet voice intoned next to Evie. That was when she realized that Hedya wasn't speaking to her but to Esther Schrock, Helen's sister, who was standing right beside her.

It was feasible that Hedya could have been talking to her. After all, Evie and Helen were best friends, but Evie, despite her crutches and obvious disabilities caused from spina bifida, seemed to somehow blend into the crowd. That was until someone needed her. They found her quickly enough then.

She supposed she shouldn't complain, but sometimes it was hard being friends with the most beautiful girl in their community. And Helen was definitely that—beautiful, even if, at the current moment, she wasn't in their community.

Her breakup with Freeman was shocking enough to all of them, but the fact that Helen had carried through with this crazy idea she had to spend a few weeks in Lancaster before deciding if she was truly ready to settle down...

That was more than Evie could comprehend.

First, the idea was unheard of. Girls didn't *decide* when they were ready to settle down. They were born ready to join the church. To find a husband and start raising adorable Amish babies. All of them in their tiny Central Pennsylvania community—with the exception of the eccentric Ada Peachy—had done exactly that. Until now.

Though Evie had no plans to marry or have children of her own. She supposed that meant the times were changing. Or maybe she was being dramatic. It wasn't that Evie didn't *want* to get married; she was simply accepting her limitations. Just as no one expected thirty-five-year-old quirky Ada Peachy to marry.

Helen had promised that she would return to Millers Creek. She had told her family that, but Evie found it hard to believe. Helen wasn't exactly testing the English world, which so often led to a person never coming back to their Amish home. Yet it was a slippery slope all the same, opting, if only for a time, for conveniences that wouldn't be accepted when she returned.

They might dress similarly, wear the same sort of prayer coverings, but there were many more differences that the Amish in Millers Creek held against the Lancaster County Amish. Millers Creek was much more conservative. No one in Evie's community used solar power in their homes, only propane to run refrigerators and hot water tanks. Evie had heard—from Helen, now that she thought about it—that the Amish women in Lancaster wore brighter colors and had decorative stitching on their dresses, even the ones for every day. It wasn't something she knew firsthand. Though she supposed Helen could confirm that when she got back. If she got back.

"She's coming home, right?" Evie said the words low so that only Esther could hear them.

Imogene Peight was standing close, and though she was a lovely woman and the salt of the earth, she was a big gossip.

"Of course she is." Esther's voice was too bright, the words too forced for Evie to completely believe her. Helen was one of her best, best friends. She had promised to return, but how could Evie truly believe that? Helen hadn't told Evie directly, and Evie found it hard to accept the blind word of another. Even if Helen had kept every other promise they had made to one another since they had become friends in the first grade.

"It's just... Freeman," Esther continued.

Evie knew that was what everyone in church was thinking.

Poor Freeman Yoder.

Freeman had never done anything in his life except love Helen Schrock. They had been no more than ten or twelve when Evie had started to notice a change in Freeman. It hadn't happened overnight, but slowly, bit by bit, it became obvious. Freeman considered all his life choices around Helen, all the plans he made, all the work he did, everything for Helen. Though Evie was trying hard not to judge harshly, she was a little annoyed with Helen for tossing all that away.

Okay, a lot annoyed. It was something she prayed about daily, asking for forgiveness and peace of heart. It wasn't her job to second-guess God's will, though at times it seemed like Helen had the world handed to her. When that ease was stacked up against the trials and setbacks that Evie faced, it was hard not to be questioning. It was hard not to wonder why.

Evie had to remind herself—*jah*, Helen was Amish, but she was also human. Like most frail and flawed humans, Helen wouldn't miss what she had while she had it. One more reason why Evie believed Helen would return as promised. For surely the glitz and commercialism of Lancaster County couldn't hold a candle to the love of a good man.

Poor Freeman Yoder.

Evie filled a couple more of the paper cups in case someone else needed a drink of water to wash down their meal, then allowed her gaze to roam around the yard in search of that familiar face. It was the first of March, the time when spring was gearing up and winter was dying down. The weather seemed to mix more and more each day. The sun was shining bright, but the wind continued to hold a bitter chill. Everyone was still wearing their coats and hats, and the women had donned their black bonnets.

Since the sun was out, they had opted to eat outside. The men had already finished, and the women were now seated around the church benches converted into tables for the meal. It didn't take her long to find Freeman among the crowd of men standing over near the barn. Because the wind was still wintry, someone had set up a small propane heater for those who might need the warmth. Barn doors were open to allow shelter for those who might need it, and children ran in and out chasing cats and dogs and puppies and kittens and chickens all through the yard.

Evie only had eyes for Freeman. As she watched, he tipped back his head and laughed like he had no care in the world. She knew his heart had to be breaking. She had talked to him a couple of times since Helen had broken up with him. At first, he had firmly believed that she was on Helen's side, and it took her a couple of attempts to convince him that she wasn't on anyone's side. Except for perhaps the side of true love. Though truth be known, if she had to pick a side it would've been Freeman's. Though she didn't like to judge.

As if sensing her gaze, Freeman turned and caught her staring at him. Evie flicked her attention elsewhere, then back. There was no sense trying to pretend she hadn't been watching him. They were friends after all.

He gave her a slight dip of his chin and took a drink of water from the little paper cup she had poured earlier. Even from the distance that separated them she could tell that his eyes held a sad light that they hadn't had before. A deepening sadness that came with each blow dealt by the woman he loved. Evie just wished she knew what to do to help them. She had tried to talk Helen out of leaving, she had tried to talk Helen out of breaking up with Freeman, she had tried to talk to Helen about anything, but all she wanted to talk about were buttons and decorative threads and fancy shoes and gray buggies. Why Helen thought gray buggies were superior to their bright yellow ones, Evie didn't know. She was just grousing at that point. So, she let it go.

She gave Freeman a sad but encouraging smile. He nodded in return, offering her a brief glimpse of his true heartache. Then he turned back to the men surrounding him and smiled once more, smiled as if all his cares had simply melted away.

Evie's heart broke a little more for her friend, and she reminded herself of Helen's promise to return. She would have to hold on to that, help Freeman hold on to it. Otherwise, they would both remain heartbroken, devastated by the loss of their friend. Evie would pray and would continue to pray that God would lead Helen back to Millers Creek. If not for Freeman's sake, then Helen's own.

"Can I give you a ride home?"

The words slipped naturally from Freeman Yoder's lips. How many times had he asked Evie if she needed a ride? Too many to count. So why did today feel different?

Because Helen was gone.

Yet that didn't make any sense to him at all.

"Aren't you..." Evie tied the large black trash bag closed and waved a hand in the general direction of the buggies.

"I brought my own buggy today," he explained, understanding her question without words.

As the sister and helper of a dairy farmer, Evie left early, and if he took her home, then he could leave early and escape all the pitying looks. He had had enough of them for one day.

Evie nodded. "*Jah*, let me tell Mattie and Naomi."

He inclined his head toward the pasture where the horses all milled around, waiting for their owners to hitch them back to their buggies and take them home. "I'll meet you at the buggies." He dipped his chin once more then turned away.

By the time he got his horse from the pasture, hitched it to his carriage and backed the rig out so he could head down the road, Evie had appeared.

He knew better than to outright ask her if she needed help getting up into the buggy. Like most of the people she rode with often, he had installed a bar to help her pull herself inside the carriage. She was strong, he knew. Years of hauling herself around on crutches and relying on her arms more than her legs had left her hardy to be sure, but still she worried him. He didn't understand why she wouldn't just let him scoop her up and place her on the carriage bench seat.

He watched her, waiting and feeling like an idiot for doing nothing as she worked to pull herself inside.

"You got it?" Freeman finally asked, despite his efforts to say and do nothing.

"I got it." She pressed her lips together, and with one last pull, she heaved herself inside the buggy.

Freeman issued a quiet sigh of relief. "Here's

a blanket." He pulled the thick wool cover up over her legs then set his horse in motion. "I still can't believe she actually did it," he said. He knew Evie would know exactly what he was referring to.

"She said she was going to," Evie reminded him.

He swallowed hard and dropped his head, the brim of his hat nearly hiding the road from in front of him. He hadn't meant to be so dramatic, but a morning of holding his head high and not letting anyone see exactly how devastated he was had done a number on his neck. "I just didn't think she would really. I mean, she broke up with me, and I figured that was cold feet or something. Rebecca said she probably wanted to make sure I really loved her. You know, like she broke up with me to make me prove my love for her."

"Rebecca needs to stop reading *Englisch* magazines when she goes to the grocery store."

He had heard a couple of the girls in their buddy bunch mention that his sister would sneak a peek at all the glossy magazines, reading articles and learning a little too much about *Englisch* ways. He knew his *vatter* would not approve, but he hadn't said anything. Nor would he. He had his own issues now.

"I did everything I could to prove that I love her. Didn't I?"

"I don't think that's the problem," Evie said.

"Then Rebecca—" Freeman stopped as Evie shook her head.

"No one knows what she's thinking, only Helen herself."

He supposed she was right. Only Helen knew her mind.

"I know what they're saying…the Schrocks. That she's coming back in a few weeks. That this is just a phase she's going through. Cold feet or something. And they believe that once she comes back she'll want to pick up right where we left off."

"And?"

The one word held the weight of the world. Of everything he held dear.

"And I don't believe that she's coming back." He didn't need to say that her staying in Lancaster would sever all ties between them. There wouldn't be a reconciliation.

"You have to trust God," Evie murmured. It was her favorite saying. He had heard her say those very words countless times. No matter how true they were, they still cut him to the bone. Trusting God meant truly accepting that she wasn't coming back. Knowing that the two of them would never get married and accepting the fact that all his dreams would have to be put on hold.

"I'm trying," he finally managed. And he was.

"God has a plan," she said, the phrase she usually uttered after the one about trusting God. Again, it was a good reminder.

"I know that too," Freeman said. "But what about when God's plan doesn't reflect your hopes and dreams? What happens then?"

"You keep going," Evie said.

It was what he had always been taught. *Man plans his way, but God directs his steps.*

"Keep going," Freeman muttered, a sigh punctuating his words. "We just had so many plans."

"The organic farm."

They had been talking about it for years. For nearly as long as they had been discussing getting married. And for Freeman those two dreams went hand in hand. They were getting married…well, they had been planning on getting married in December. Before then, he would buy a farm. He had already been looking. Then together they would certify it as organic and grow all sorts of vegetables to sell and can. Mostly for the *Englischers* who swore by organic products.

"William Hostetler is selling his farm," he said quietly.

"Are you serious?" Evie spun in her seat, nearly knocking the blanket off her lap in the process.

William Hostetler had one of the most successful organic farms in the area.

"Rumor has it he and his wife Adele are moving to Indiana so they can be closer to their daughter-in-law when the grandkids start coming."

"His farm is perfect for you."

She was right. The farm *was* perfect. Having it already certified organic would take a lot of work off him. *If* he decided to go ahead with all his plans. He was struggling, that was certain. One minute he was raring to go and the next he wanted to crawl under the bed and never come out again. He supposed it would get better with time. He hoped it would anyway.

"We were supposed to go look at it tomorrow," Freeman continued.

"You should still go."

"I don't know." He hated the negativity in his voice. "If she's not here…"

"I know you two shared the dream, but if I'm remembering correctly, it was your original idea, was it not?"

"Jah." He swallowed hard. "But now—"

Evie shook her head. "Now you're going to go look at the farm. Maybe buy it before anyone else can. That farm won't stay on the market until Helen makes up her mind, one way or the other. You still have a life to live, and if you are planning on living it here, you might as well be living out the dream you've been dreaming half your life."

He was taken aback at her pointed words and tone. But Evie wasn't finished.

"If Helen is dumb enough to stay in Lancaster, then she doesn't deserve to live the life you dreamed about. And you surely shouldn't give up on it too. At the very least, you should go look at the farm."

"I've already seen it once," he admitted.

She nodded understandingly. "Tomorrow you were going to take Helen with you and show her."

"If she liked it, then I was going to put down some money on it. You know, in good faith."

"You have the money to buy the farm?"

"Most of it," he said.

"That's impressive."

"Dat said he would help with the rest."

"Then you have to do it," she said. "Don't worry about Helen, or what she's doing. You have to buy the farm before someone else swoops in and snatches it away."

He thought about it a moment. It truly was a beautiful piece of land. He would enjoy seeing it again. Especially with Evie at his side. "Okay," he said. "I'll do it. Please say you'll come with me."

"Jah," Evie said. "Of course."

Chapter Two

"So, I've been thinking…" Evie started. Was she really going to do this? *Jah*. She definitely was. "I want to try milking the goats."

She had been thinking about it for a while. More than her sisters knew.

More than anything in the world she wanted independence. She wanted a little house all her own, some acreage in the back and her very own goats. She didn't want to make cheese like her sister. It was too time-consuming. Plus, she didn't want to be in competition with her kin. Instead, she would make goat milk soaps and lotions to sell at all the little markets throughout the valley. That would pay for her house and allow her to be on her own, dependent on no one.

Their father, Thomas Ebersol, had raised all six of his girls to be strong and independent. Maybe because they lost their mother at such an early age. Mattie, the oldest, had just turned eighteen, while the youngest, Sarah Ann, was barely six. When Mattie's husband, David, passed away, Naomi and Evie had come to stay and help their pregnant sister with her two little girls and the herd of goats.

"You want to help?" Mattie raised one brow in question. Evie could see the surprise on her sister's face. She'd never milked the goats. It had always been her job to stay inside and take care of the children.

"Yes. I want to learn how." It took all the gumption she had to say the words. It was one thing to have a dream and another to share it with people who, though they loved her very much, seemed to constantly remind her of her disabilities. She knew they meant well. Whenever they were all together Evie always got the chore best suited to her capabilities, or lack thereof. How was she supposed to stretch and grow if she was never allowed the opportunity?

"Evie, you can't milk the goats," Naomi said as she came down the stairs.

Evie turned to glare at her sister. "I surely will never be able to if I never try."

"They can be quite…ornery," Mattie said, definitely more diplomatic than Naomi. Still.

Evie had spent the whole afternoon talking to Freeman about pursuing his dreams, and yet she had done nothing to pursue her own. *Jah*, she'd had to adjust her dream to fit her life. God had a plan, and she had a purpose. Now she needed to see it through.

"I know the goats can be overly playful," Evie started. She wanted to downplay the mischievousness of the goats a tad. After all, she needed a more positive attitude in order to make her dreams a reality. The goats were ornery. The goats were playful. But she could handle them. That was something she had to believe. "But I'll do just fine."

Naomi stood at the bottom of the staircase, mouth hanging open.

Mattie hovered at the door, looking back and forth between Naomi and Evie, apparently trying to find something to say.

"Why?" The one word was like a bullet from a hunting rifle.

"I…" She could do this. They were her sisters. They would understand, support her even. "I want a small goat farm of my own," she finally admitted.

Naomi made a noise behind her, but Evie ignored it and concentrated instead on Mattie's curious expression.

"Go on," Mattie urged.

Evie spilled it all right there. How she would

milk goats, make soaps and lotions and some-how finally gain her independence.

Once she finished she waited, near breath-less for Mattie to comment.

Finally, she spoke. "Get your sweater and let's go." Without another word she opened the front door and stepped out into the chilly spring afternoon. Mattie expertly blocked the door so that Charlie, her more than ornery and more than a little playful pygmy goat, couldn't run outside. Once the beast hit the outdoors, she was nearly impossible to catch.

Evie wasted no time, grabbing a covering and closing the front door firmly on Charlie's indignant bleat before following her sister out to the goat barn.

She might normally be the one left inside to watch the girls, but she had been in the barn countless times since she had come to stay with Mattie. Still, when she opened the door to the barn, she looked at it with new eyes.

Like most milking barns, this one was set up with feed troughs to distract the animal from what was going on. Unlike a regular dairy barn, there was a raised platform for them to stand on, so they were easier to reach, and a hook to hold the goat in place.

Mattie opened the door to the outside pen

and allowed half of the herd inside. The goats on the opposite side of the door bleated, knowing that they'd been cut off from dinner. The rest merrily hopped up onto their platforms, stuck their heads through the holders and began to eat.

"Grab that milker over there," Mattie said, pointing toward the vacuum-powered milk extractor hanging on the wall.

Evie nodded and moved toward it.

"There's really not much to it," Mattie explained. "Use the antiseptic solution to clean their teat, then slip the milking tube on each one and pump the milk. You have to be kind of quick though because the goats get bored easily and then you'll have them fighting to get out."

"Right," Evie said. She could do this.

The milk extractor was hung too high for her to reach, but she wasn't about to ask for assistance. She would work through it, figure it out on her own.

In her own milking parlor, she would have the equipment where she could reach it herself. No biggie.

For now…she braced her crutches against the wall and pulled on the milking device. All the while, she was doing her best to keep it from falling on her head and to somehow keep herself from falling backward—while simultaneously trying to hurry because the goats were already getting impatient.

She heard Mattie moving behind her and had the feeling that her sister was on to the next goat. Yet Evie hadn't even managed to retrieve the equipment.

She could do this.

Lifting herself up as tall as possible was no help. Finally, Evie grabbed one of her crutches and used it to push up the weight of the milking device and pop it off the hook. Thankfully, she caught it.

She wanted to take a small moment to celebrate her victory. She was very proud of herself for having reclaimed the device, but she was certain that Mattie was on her fourth or fifth goat.

"Pride goeth before the fall…" she muttered and slipped her arms back through the cuffs of her crutches and eyed the milking device. Now all she had to do was get it over to the goats. She bit back a sigh.

If she kept it up at this rate, she wouldn't even get one goat milked before her sister was done with all the rest of them. That was *not* what she wanted.

And she had thought she could come out here and do this whole chore by herself.

Still, she wasn't giving up. Somehow she managed to drag both her crutches and herself and the milking device over to the carousel where the goats waited—some patiently, some impatiently—to be milked. There were only a handful of goats still left.

She could do this.

But the goat was resistant to her efforts, dancing to one side as Evie tried to clean her teats. Evie was half afraid she was going to hurt the animal but noticed that Mattie had no compunction. Her sister grabbed the goat and washed her with confidence, keeping one hand in place as she reached for the milking device.

Confidence. That was what Mattie had that she didn't. But after several unsuccessful tries, it became increasingly apparent that there was a measure of skill and practice involved as well.

That will come with time, she told herself. But if she took too long, then the house she had chosen would belong to someone else and her dream would have to start all over again. She had to make sure that didn't happen.

"Are you doing okay over there?" Mattie asked from the other side of the carousel.

"Fine," Evie fibbed, running the back of her sleeve across her forehead. She was going to have to get into better shape if she was going to milk goats for a living. And she was. She was determined.

Evie set her chin and moved to the next goat. "Are you ready for the next round?"

That was when she realized that she had only managed to milk three goats in the time it took Mattie to do the rest. "Almost." She said the word in the most chipper tone she had. She was not about to let this get her down. She was determined.

She could do this. Half the problem the first go-round was getting the actual machine off the wall. That was already accomplished.

Evie also noticed that Mattie had taken her buckets of milk and deposited them in the cooler for her. That was a chore she was going to have to find a better solution for. Perhaps next week she could find the time to head into town to the library and research it on the computers they had there. There were over eight billion people on the planet. Surely she wasn't the only person with a disability who wanted to own a goat farm.

She was winded and tired and ready to sit down by the time they finished the last goat and sent her into the play barn. Evie couldn't wait to get inside and put her feet up for a bit. The milking had been more work than she had anticipated, but her herd wouldn't be as large, and she would have a couple of months of practice before she made the switch. She would be fine.

She adjusted her shawl and turned toward the door of the milking parlor. That was when she noticed Mattie wasn't right behind her.

"Are you coming?"

Her sister was standing at the sink, running the water and testing it with her fingers to make sure it was warm enough. "*Jah*. I just have to clean the milking devices."

The cleanup. She inwardly sighed. She hadn't thought about that. Hadn't counted on it as she figured it was her time to get into the house and rest up a bit.

Carefully she made her way to her sister's side. Evie leaned her crutches against the far edge of the stainless steel sink and rolled up her sleeves. *Jah*, it was a lot more work than she had anticipated, but she could do it. After all, she had God on her side.

"Freeman, is that you?"

"*Jah*," he called in return. He sat down on the bench in the mudroom and started unlacing his boots.

"*Jah?*" Suddenly his mother appeared in

the doorway that led into their large family kitchen. Ever since Helen had told him that she wanted out of their engagement, his mother had been so diligent in watching out for him. Almost to the point that Freeman felt like he was six years old again.

"Did you talk to Evie?" Mamm asked. Charity Yoder Yoder—yes, two Yoders. She was a Yoder before she got married and a Yoder after she got married. Yoder was a common name after all—wiped her hands on a dishtowel and eyed him with earnest attention.

Freeman began to work on his other boot but nodded at his *mamm*. *"Jah."*

"What did she say?" Mamm asked. "That Evie's a sweet bird."

He didn't need her to tell him what kind of person Evie Ebersol was. He had known Evie most of his life, and he had always known her to be honest and true and loving and godly. A man couldn't ask for more in his best friend. *Jah*, that was what Evie was to him. His best friend. Her and Helen. Then Helen had done an about-face and now nothing seemed to be the same. Not even Evie. Which made him believe that he was the one who was changing. He was the one who was seeing things with different eyes.

"She says Helen promised to come back." It was all Freeman could manage. It still stuck in his craw to know that she could come back, upholding her promise to return. Yet she hadn't promised to come back and marry him.

He had spent so much of his life knowing that he was going to marry Helen Schrock. It was unfathomable to believe anything else. Yet that was right where he found himself.

"She said as much to you as well," his *mamm* reminded him.

As if he needed reminding.

He made a show of straightening his boots and putting them in order with the rest of the family's shoes, lined up against the far wall of the mudroom. He wanted the time to compose his features, get himself set and put on the happy face that everyone expected from him. He turned back to his mother and smiled. "It's in God's hands," he said, quoting Evie as he padded in his sock feet past her and into the kitchen.

On Sundays in their community, there was no big meal prepared. Somehow it fell into the category of unnecessary and excessive work for a Sabbath. So as usual, the table was set with a platter of cold cuts and cheese, crackers, olives, pickles and applesauce. Chowchow and all sorts of relishes were available to them, as well as a bag of store-bought chips and a loaf of day-old homemade bread.

He should be grateful. He had food to eat and a roof over his head, but he just didn't feel like eating. He knew it was probably his dissatisfaction with Helen bleeding over into his everyday life. What was a guy to do? All he had ever wanted was to marry Helen, buy the organic farm and live happily ever after.

Jah, there would be trials and such through their lives. He knew that; he understood it. God's will could be a difficult thing to comprehend, so perhaps happily ever after was relative. Perhaps as happy as possible ever after, or something like that.

He shook his head at himself and did his best to straighten out his own thoughts.

Despite what she said, he knew Helen was not coming back. The allure of Lancaster County would be her downfall.

Too many times he'd heard her talk about buttons and stitches and fabrics she wished she could wear. He didn't understand the difference in it all, but it had meant something to her. Something more that he couldn't comprehend or compete with. She wanted that lifestyle.

Flowers in the yards, the staid gray buggies, the solar panels that her kin had.

Why would she come back to boring Millers Creek when she could be there? What was organic farming when compared to working in the stores that she had shown him in the travel brochures her cousins had sent? No. She was never coming back. Which meant he couldn't put his life on hold for her.

That was not something he was willing to do. Starting tomorrow. Tomorrow he and Evie were going to look at the Hostetler farm, and it would be his first step in a new life without Helen Schrock. The only thing he could do now was move forward. He wasn't sure exactly how, but that was the plan. Onward.

"Well, boy, what do you think?" William Hostetler ended his tour just outside of the barn.

Evie rested against the fence surrounding the horse corral as the men gazed out over what was essentially a very large garden. Growing a single organic crop was different than growing a variety of fruits and vegetables that would eventually be sold at a farmers market. Even with nothing planted, the differences were apparent. There were rows designated for corn next to rows designated for squash next to the bed saved for strawberries and so forth and so on. Yet there was one thing undeniable about the Hostetler farm: it was gorgeous. Like everything else in the valley, it was sprawling, yet somehow cozy, lush and starting to turn green, beautifully sun-kissed as the rays poured down from the sky.

She didn't want to talk badly about her friend, not even in her own thoughts. But Helen was a fool. The farm was magnificent, so peaceful, and Helen would have been sharing it with Freeman Yoder. Evie simply couldn't fathom how anything could hold charm over being married to Freeman, living here and praising God. What more could a woman ask for?

If she were being fair, she couldn't hold that dream for herself. Perhaps that was how Helen felt about it as well. It was a lovely dream, but one she couldn't make her own.

The thought had barely crossed her mind when Hostetler's horse came ambling across the small corral. The men dickered back and forth, but Evie was hardly paying attention.

The mare chuffed as she drew near the trio. Obviously sensing the men were not going to pay her any mind, she approached Evie.

"Hey, there, big girl." Evie took her arm out of the cuff of her right-side crutch and rubbed the mare's velvety nose. The beast nodded her head in appreciation. Evie cooed nonsensical words to her as she stroked her snout and let the men's words wash past her. Peaceful, serene, almost drifting away into another world, Evie continued to stroke the horse. Then Freeman said something that jarred her back to reality.

"I'll take it."

Evie swung around to stare gape-mouthed at her friend. "You're...you're buying the farm? Like right now?" She stopped, staring at him with wide eyes. "I mean, this is a surprise."

"It's time, don't you think?" Freeman flashed her a bright smile, but his eyes were unreadable.

Not true. They were readable, but all she could see was happiness and a sense of satisfaction that the first part of his dream was becoming a reality. She could only suppose that he wasn't worried too much about whether or not Helen was coming back home and whether or not she would marry him when she got there. What had changed his mind?

Perhaps he would explain on the way home.

She felt a nudge on her shoulder and turned, realizing the mare wanted more attention. Evie gave her a couple more courtesy pats and switched her attention back to the pair of men in front of her.

"I'm glad," Hostetler was saying. "I'm glad

it's going to a fine young person like yourself."
He clapped Freeman on the shoulder as if the
pair were longtime friends.

"I'll bring you the money by this afternoon?"
It was half a question from Freeman with a little bit of statement mixed in.

"Fine, fine."

This afternoon? Was this really happening? How she wished she could get Freeman
by himself. Just to be sure he was making the
right decision. He could be a little headstrong
at times. She had seen it plenty, and she could
only hope he wasn't jumping into something
more than he could handle just to prove that he
could. To show everyone in Miller Creek that
he truly was moving on without Helen.

There was another possible reason that he
was buying the farm so quickly and without
Helen: to encourage her to come back. To show
her his success in hopes that she would return.
Just the thought made Evie a little queasy.

"Freeman," she started. Another nudge at her
shoulder, but this one she ignored. "I thought
you were going to think about it."

Both men stared at her as if she had lost her
mind. Who was she to be asking? Not his intended. Not someone he was going to share his

life with. Just a girl who could barely stand on her own two feet.

"I mean—" Evie had to grab the fence to keep from falling over. The horse had decided the attention needed to be on her and not the men. The mare headbutted Evie in the shoulder—hard. Needy horse or not, Evie wanted to know. "Are you sure you want to do this *now*?" She retrieved her crutch and moved a little farther from the fence.

"It's my dream, Evie. I'm moving forward."

Without Helen. She should be proud, but she hoped he wasn't moving too fast. Too much change was hard on the heart. But she also knew that he had been saving his money since he got out of school. And she knew that his father had promised to help him with the rest. The money was there and waiting.

Hostetler cleared his throat. "We still got a deal?"

For one hard moment, Freeman continued to stare at her, then he turned back to the farm owner. *"Jah,"* he said. "We still have a deal."

"What just happened here?" Evie moved along beside him, her crutches clinking as she hurried to keep up.

Freeman slowed his steps, realizing that he was walking too fast for his friend.

After he made the deal with William Hostetler, the two men shook hands, and now Freeman and Evie were headed back to his buggy. The bright yellow seemed extra cheery today, gleaming like a fresh-bloomed flower in the clear March sun.

"I told you yesterday."

"Yesterday, you said you wanted to look at the farm. I didn't realize you were seriously considering buying it *today*."

"So, it would have been okay if I'd bought it tomorrow instead?" he joked. This was his dream, and if he wanted it, he had to get it whether Helen was there or not. Surely Evie could understand that.

He wasn't sure how he came up with the idea that organic farming was his calling, but once he had it, it stuck. He was the youngest son in his family, so he wasn't going to inherit the Yoder farm anytime soon. Aside from the fact that his father was still a relatively young fifty-seven, his older brothers, Jonas and Luke, still lived at home.

Freeman also had to take into account the organic certification. It wasn't an easy task to come by such a listing, and converting a farm that had been running non-organically to a certified organic farm took a great deal of work. It would possibly be years before he could turn a decent profit on such a venture. That was what made this place so ideal.

Besides, he loved everything about this farm. The way it looked, the way it smelled. It was perfect.

At first he had believed that the farm would be nothing without Helen…without a partner. But Evie had said it all yesterday—if he didn't jump on it now, he might miss it altogether.

"I mean…" Evie trailed off, apparently at a loss to explain her own motivations.

"I thought you would be happy for me."

She stopped next to the buggy and practically wilted with what he supposed was some degree of shame. "I'm sorry. I didn't mean it that way. I just want to make sure that you're making the right decision here."

Freeman gave a confident nod. "I am. Either way this is my dream and I'm gonna make it a reality." *With or without Helen* was implied but not said. He could see the understanding light in Evie's sweet hazel eyes.

She took a moment, seemingly thinking it over before giving him a small dip of her chin. "Okay. I guess. *Jah.*"

She didn't seem sure at all.

"Now, what's wrong with you?" Freeman asked.

She turned and made her way around the buggy to the passenger side. He waited for her to hoist herself into the carriage before expecting her answer. Somehow in the whole transaction he managed to bite back his offer to help. Maybe because he was so entwined in his own thoughts, it didn't occur to him until she was already seated.

"Nothing," she said.

Yet still, Freeman thought something had to be wrong.

Was it Helen? He knew that Helen's leaving had a ripple effect in the community, hurting those close around her more as the shock worked its way outward. Evie was one of those close to the center.

"Now, why don't I believe that?" Freeman waved one last time to William Hostetler, who was standing on the porch watching them, though thankfully out of earshot.

"Believe what you like," Evie said.

For the life of him, Freeman couldn't figure out what had gotten into her.

Women. He would never understand them. He'd heard that said often enough and now he believed it to be true.

He started the buggy for the road, deciding it better to leave Evie stewing in her own thoughts than press the issue further.

Normally the silence between him and Evie was comfortable. True, he couldn't say this was necessarily *uncomfortable*, but there was definitely something itchy about the whole thing. He could feel her doubts, or maybe they were misgivings, some sort of emotion she was giving off that made him start to doubt his own choices. It was something he didn't want to do, and he didn't understand. Normally, Evie was completely on his side, always supportive and earnest in helping. Yet today, something seemed off.

Once again, he decided to leave the matter for another time. There was no sense riling her up over nothing. Plus, he had what he wanted. He had shaken hands on buying the Hostetler organic farm. The responsibility wouldn't be without its trials and hardships, and it was going to be difficult to go it alone. He would much rather have someone at his side, helping him, but he couldn't make Helen come back. He felt almost too old and worn out to try to find love with someone else. No, it might be better to go into this venture alone, make it his own. Not worry about another soul. Then see what God had planned.

They rode along, side by side, and Freeman started to get the impression that maybe Evie did have something she wanted to say. The closer they came to her house, the more it seemed she wanted to share whatever it was that was building up inside her. Once she even opened her mouth to speak, then shut it and settled back down in her seat. He so badly wanted to ask her what she had been about to say, but he knew if he did, she would brush him off. If he wanted to know what was on her mind, he would have to wait until she was ready to speak it.

Of course, with everything going on at the moment, patience was his best virtue. Yet he had to almost bite his tongue to keep from talking about it as they drove along.

"Look," he said, pointing toward the school playground as they started past. He did it more to distract himself than he did to show Evie, but he loved driving by and watching the children play. He loved seeing that big old tree in the yard standing tall and true. The very same tree where he had met Evie for the first time.

He supposed he had seen her before, maybe at church, but she was a girl, and he wasn't going to go talk to her. But something that day at school drew him to her. First day of the first grade. Even though Evie had Mattie at school with her, Evie was sitting all alone.

Freeman remembered that day like it was yesterday. Evie plucking at the grass and clover she sat on, acting as though she was perfectly content to be all alone. A person just had to look at her to see that that wasn't the case. In hindsight, he now realized his assessment had been very intuitive for a six-year-old. It wasn't something he could've verbalized at the time, simply something he knew in his gut. Or maybe it was his heart. Despite her aloof attitude and the haughty angle of her lifted chin, he plopped down next to her while everyone else ran and played.

"Do you remember—" He broke off, not sure exactly how to recall that day. What were the words he needed? He didn't know. Words seemed too small. That day had been more than *when we sat under the tree together in first grade*. Or *that day when I first talked to you*. Or even *the time when I asked you to marry me*.

The thought surprised him, and he jerked back on the reins. The horse chuffed and shook her head, showing her displeasure with his misdirection.

"Easy, girl," he murmured to the mare, trying to get them both back on track.

That day was etched into his mind so deeply that he had almost forgotten it, if that was even possible. It was just a day that had been. He didn't pick apart its individual pieces. Now that he was thinking about it, it was the day when he had told Evie that if neither one of them was married by the age of twenty-two then he would marry her. They would live happily ever after on a big farm.

"I proposed to you." He shot her a sideways grin.

He wasn't sure where the number twenty-two came from. He supposed that as a six-year-old, it might've been his favorite number at the time. Who knew?

Evie pulled the blanket up a little bit closer around her and gave a small nod. "That you did."

"Those were the days, huh?" He hadn't meant for his voice to turn quite so soft or quite so wistful, but there it was. Those were the times when they couldn't wait to grow up, and now that they were grown-up, they wished they hadn't wished their lives away. He supposed that was all part of growing up, all part of being a child. Though he had to admit, Evie had seemed too old for her age even then.

"I felt like such an outsider."

It might've been the last thing he expected her to say. How could she have felt like an outsider? Such a close-knit community, loving family, meddlesome church district. Nobody was left alone too long in Millers Creek. Yet her chin had taken on a sad curve, and her lips pressed together.

He looked at her for as long as he dared then glanced back at the road. "What about now?"

"Nee." But she hesitated too long before she said the word, and he knew she wasn't telling the complete truth. It wasn't like Evie to lie. Not about anything. He supposed some things were too personal to share.

She felt like an outsider? The thought broke his heart.

Evie seemed to realize her mistake and mumbled, "Sometimes," backpedaling on her original answer.

He knew she was downplaying her troubles. She was the kindest person he knew, and she deserved everything in the world, all of God's good blessings. She helped people when they needed it. She had always been there for him.

Then that proposal…

He kept running it through his mind over and over. Marrying Evie Ebersol. Funny how he'd made that promise all those years ago and was only now remembering it. And on the day that he bought his farm. On the day she rode out with him to look at his farm. It had to be some kind of sign from God, a way to show them the path.

"Do you remember what I said to you that day?" he asked.

She drew back and eyed him warily, a small frown forming between her dark brows. He wasn't certain but he suspected she was stalling for time. "Didn't we just cover this?"

"Specifically," he clarified.

"You...you said that if we weren't married by twenty-two that you would marry me," she finally admitted. "I told you I didn't think I would ever get married. How did we get on that subject anyway?" she asked. "We were six years old."

He shook his head, not really sure himself. "I think we were talking about growing up, and the things that we were going to do." How they were going to run everything, be the boss of the house, get to do what they wanted.

Jah, that all came true.

He was watching the road ahead of him, but he could feel her gaze on him, studying his features, outlining each shade of his expression.

Finally, she turned away and faced forward, adjusting the blanket over her legs and folding her hands primly over the top. "Well, that was a long time ago."

Was he really thinking about this?

"*Jah*, it was."

Helen had walked away from everything that they had planned together. Everything that they had wanted and dreamed of for years. Who knew if she would ever come back? Sometimes, like now, he didn't even care if she did.

Okay…it'd only been a couple of days, but the stress of it all was beginning to eat at his insides and he was done with that. He didn't like it. It wasn't fun. It was too much.

And Evie… Evie had always been there. Evie was true-blue, as they say. She was loyal and honest and godly, such a beautiful person inside and out. She deserved so much better than what life had handed her. *Jah*. They were taught to accept God's will and move forward, but sometimes it was hard not to think *Why me?* Evie never seemed to stumble over those words. She simply kept moving along, kept being Evie, kept smiling. *Jah*, she deserved more.

That alone was reason to follow through with his promise to her. Because of all the people he had known in his life, she had never once led him astray or hurt him, either intentionally or on accident. She had the purest heart he knew.

"A promise is a promise," he said. He hadn't meant his voice to crack on the last word, or for them to sound slightly choked as they hit the air. It was just the idea, the thought, of marrying Evie. *Jah*, he liked it.

Evie let out a nervous laugh. "Freeman, be serious. We were six years old."

"A promise is a promise, Evie." His voice had gained more confidence, and Freeman sat up a little straighter in his seat.

"Twenty-two came and went a long time ago," she said, shifting, playing with the blanket and then primly folding her hands across her lap once again.

"Are you saying you're going to break your promise to me?"

She whirled around to stare at him, her mouth hanging slightly open. "I promised no such thing."

He turned in her direction casually, as if they were talking about what to have for dinner instead of getting married. "You did so. We made a deal, a pact, remember? We shook hands on it."

She closed her eyes and shook her head.

"Freeman, seriously," she finally said. "We were six."

He shrugged and returned his attention to the road. Yes, twenty-two had come and gone, and they hadn't been married then. Because he hadn't thought about it then. Because he had planned on marrying Helen. As far as he was concerned, there was no reason to think about a promise he had made twenty years ago. But now...now everything was different. Now Helen was gone, twenty-two was gone and Evie was still here. The more he thought about marrying Evie, living with her on the farm, the more it made sense.

"You need to stop," she said. She laid a sweet hand on his arm, beseeching him with the one touch.

"We promised each other," he said.

Evie shook her head. "This is one promise you don't have to keep."

Chapter Three

"Sister? Are you in here?"

Evie snatched a dish towel from the counter and quickly dried her hands before making her way to the kitchen door. *"Jah,"* she replied. "What are you doing here?"

Sarah Ann Ebersol, the youngest of Evie's sisters, somehow managed to shrug her shoulders and take off her coat at the same time. Evie was certain that the action was meant to look casual, but she knew her sister too well. Sarah Ann didn't look her in the eyes. Her gaze was downcast as she hung up her coat then turned to face Evie. "Nothing much," she said.

"I see," Evie replied. "Would you like some buttermilk pie? Naomi made one this morning."

Sarah Ann shook her head, a sad wagging back and forth.

"Oh, dear," Evie said. She had never known Sarah Ann to turn down buttermilk pie. It was her absolute favorite. "How about we sit down?" She nodded toward the couch where Charlie, the goat, was already lounging, waiting for Mattie's daughters to come back in and play.

Evie settled herself down into the one armchair, allowing Sarah Ann to perch on the couch next to Charlie. She waited patiently for her sister to begin.

She didn't like to say that she was accustomed to this, but somehow, she had become something of a fixer in their family, perhaps even in the church district. It seemed that someone was always coming to her for advice about one thing or another. Evie wasn't sure how the trend got started. She supposed it was because she was always on the sidelines. She was always regulated to watching, and in watching, she noticed things that others might have missed.

She waited a few moments more and was about to say something when Sarah Ann spoke. "It's just that…" She trailed off, her fingers nervously pleating the fabric of her apron.

Evie waited. Her sister would get there eventually. Rushing her would only make her more nervous, and she was clearly distressed about whatever it was that she came to talk about.

Patience is a virtue, everyone knew that, and

Evie had bucketloads. Again, possibly a side effect of always being on the fringes.

"Noah Peight asked if he could take me home from the next singing." The words rushed out of her, then Sarah Ann released a hefty sigh.

"Okay," Evie said when she realized Sarah Ann was once again stalled. "This is a problem?" The words fell somewhere between inquiry and statement, and Evie let them hang there, suspended as Sarah Ann nodded miserably.

"Why is that?" Evie prodded.

"He's so old." Finally, Sarah Ann lifted her head. Her hands rose and fell back into her lap, her eyes filled with tears.

"I see." Evie shifted in her seat. She wouldn't exactly call Noah Peight *old*. He was twenty-five. Though when compared in Sarah Ann's eyes to her own eighteen, Evie was certain he seemed practically ancient. "I take it you don't fancy Noah."

Sarah Ann shook her head glumly.

"Does this have anything to do with Judah Peachy?"

"No. Maybe. No."

Evie smiled gently at her sister. "I can't help you if you won't talk to me about it. I assume you did come here to talk to me about it. *Jah?*"

Sarah Ann sucked in a deep, fortifying breath. "It's Lizzie." Once again tears welled in her blue eyes.

"Lizzie? How did she get involved in this?" It was almost a dumb question. Their sister Lizzie seemed to be involved in everything. It wasn't that she was a busybody. She was sort of a social butterfly. Flitting around, seemingly having her fingers in pie after pie. One of the things she loved most of all was teasing Sarah Ann. As Evie waited for her sister to answer, she had a feeling that was the problem.

"She told me that if I didn't go home with him, I would probably never get married." The words rushed out of Sarah Ann in a tone very near a wail, and a few tears slipped down her cheeks.

Married. Why did the one word bring back memories of Freeman's proposal? Especially when it was something that she had no business thinking about. Not when her sister needed her. And definitely not when they all knew she was the sister that would never get married.

Evie pushed herself forward in the armchair and reached out a hand to her sister. "Lizzie is teasing you, and you know it. She's terrible about that." She meant no harm, of that Evie was 100 percent certain. Lizzie simply had a mischievous streak to go along with her ener-getic nature. Sometimes for a gentle soul like Sarah Ann it could be almost too much to han-dle.

Sarah Ann's knee began to bounce, though she managed to draw in the rest of her tears. For now, anyway. "I know that. But what if she's right?"

"Oh, honey," Evie crooned, rubbing a thumb across the back of her sister's soft hand. "You know that's not true."

"But I don't."

Evie sighed. "Whatever happens, it's God's will." It was the best counsel she could offer her truly. Whatever happened was God's will. The best thing to do was accept it and go on. It was a fact that she had to remind herself of nearly every day.

"I guess so." Sarah Ann pulled her hand from Evie's grasp and started plucking at an invisible spot on her apron.

"You know so," Evie corrected. "I think this has more to do with Judah Peachy than you're letting on."

Pick. Pick. Pick. "Maybe."

It was a conversation they had had before, and Evie wasn't sure if she had anything new to add to it today. Judah Peachy had turned eighteen, then left his Amish upbringing behind. It was almost as if he had disappeared. No one had heard from him in the two years he'd been gone.

Sarah Ann had been a tender sixteen, newly able to attend singings, and she had set her sights on Judah. Then he was gone.

The weekly singings were more than just a fun and simple way for them to spend their Sunday evenings. Everyone knew that it was the best place to find their future spouse. Where she came from, most married someone from their community, their church district even. The singings were where all that took place.

If there was one thing Evie knew about her sister, it was that Sarah Ann loved deeply. It was going to take a lot to shake her of the idea of Judah as her husband.

There'd been all sorts of rumors about what Judah was out doing in the *Englisch* world. Some that even included him living in a different Amish community. No one knew for certain. If he was telling his parents or his close friends where he was, they weren't telling anyone else. A person had to assume that he had sent no word. It looked very much like he was never coming back.

"Lizzie is only teasing you, but you have to realize, if you stay hung up on Judah Peachy then it won't be teasing and will be more of a prophecy."

Sarah Ann raised those baby blue eyes to meet hers. "I guess you're right. I mean, you're right. I know it. What am I supposed to do now? Marry Noah Peight?"

Evie pushed down her own emotions regarding the situation. They would not be productive to share, but if Noah Peight had asked her, Evie, to go home from a singing, she wouldn't have thought twice about it. He was handsome and had a good job. He was kind and godly, and like Freeman Yoder, he was perfect husband material. But he wouldn't ask Evie if he could take her home from a singing, and if he did, she would have to tell him no as well. She wasn't getting married. She had already accepted that as God's will. It was the very same reason why she couldn't accept Freeman's proposal no matter how badly she wanted to.

"If you don't want to ride home with Noah Peight, then don't do it. He apparently likes you, and you don't want to get his hopes up if you don't feel the same."

Sarah Ann nodded. "You're right, of course."

"And ignore Lizzie. She's teasing you. You know she loves you or she wouldn't tease you."

"Sometimes I wish she didn't love me quite so much," Sarah Ann mumbled.

Evie chuckled at her sister's small joke. "The last singing we were all at together, I noticed Mose King looking your way an awful lot."

Sarah Ann tilted her head to one side as if contemplating the idea. Mose King was definitely closer to Sarah Ann's age, and though he wasn't quite yet grown into husband material, he came from a good family. The Kings were well-known in their church district, though Mose was considered to be a little bit of a troublemaker. Not bad, but definitely testing the borders of his *rumspringa*. Everyone believed he would settle down soon, and if the looks he was casting at Sarah Ann were any indication, she would be the one to help him do that. Now if Evie could just steer them both in the right direction.

"Mose King," Sarah Ann murmured to herself, as if trying it out for the future. Then she gave a small nod, and a bright smile chased away her tears. "I love you, Evie. You're the best," she said. She knelt on the floor in front of Evie and wrapped her in a tight hug, pressing the side of her face against Evie's heart.

Evie smoothed down the edge of Sarah Ann's prayer *kapp*. "I love you too, sister."

"So, I did it." Freeman looked around the table at the members of his family. He had waited until everyone was seated for supper, the silent prayer had been offered and everyone was filling their plates before sharing his news.

The table had been filled with chatter. It was no wonder, seeing as how there were seven people seated around it with Freeman's dad, Andy, at its head.

His *dat* swallowed the bite he had taken as he was filling his plate and cleared his throat before pinning his son with his concentrated stare. "You did what, son?"

Freeman felt a little bit of his excitement leak out of him like a balloon with a tiny hole in it. Honestly, he couldn't believe that his *dat* didn't remember. It had been all that Freeman had talked about. Until Helen decided to break up with him and leave town. Once that happened that was all anyone could talk about.

"The farm. I told you the other day that William Hostetler is selling his organic farm."

From the opposite end of the table, his mother, Charity, cleared her throat. All attention swiveled to her, but she continued to spoon applesauce onto her plate next to her thick slice of ham. Then she passed the jar on to his sister Rebecca.

"I suppose I should say he *was* selling it," Freeman corrected. "I bought it today. So, I guess it's not for sale any longer."

"Did Helen come back?" His sister Claire sat up a little straighter in her seat, looking around at the other members of the family.

"Claire!" Rebecca whispered. Even Jonas and Luke ducked their heads. Rebecca could be that way, Freeman supposed. She was the oldest daughter but trapped in the middle of the Andy Yoder pecking order.

Claire sank back into her chair. "I didn't know. I'm at the school with the children all day. How am I supposed to find these things out?"

"It's all right, Claire," Freeman said. "Helen didn't come back." He said the words with only the smallest pang of sadness. More like regret than real sorrow. "But I'm going ahead with my plans to buy the farm and start a life." He wanted to add *with Evie Ebersol* to that sentence, but he needed to talk to her again first. It didn't matter that they were six years old when they made their vow. It didn't matter that twenty-two was four years ago. He had been caught up with Helen then and now…

Well, now, he could only see Helen's change of heart to be a blessing from above. God stepping in and showing him what He had really planned for Freeman. Apparently, Evie too.

"I see." His father took his time buttering the fluffy yeasty rolls that his mom always served when they had ham for supper.

The mouthwatering aroma of those rolls was enough to send his stomach growling on any given day, and today was no different. Yet Freeman's roll sat unattended on the side of his plate, half on his ham and half on his green beans. No butter in sight. And there was something in his father's tone that made him stop still, delicious roll forgotten.

"We're still on, right?" Freeman asked, hating that his voice sounded a little shaky. He was moving forward, and now for some reason he felt like he was doing something wrong. "You can still help me with the payments?" Again, he wished his voice sounded stronger, that his tone hadn't tilted up on the end, making his statement into a question.

His father shook his head and set his knife down carefully. "Money is not the issue, son. We were thinking you would be here for this year's harvest."

Freeman recalled then, his father had said

something to him during those first few days after Helen had dropped her exploding news. The wedding was off, and she hinted to her plans to go to Lancaster. His father had asked him then what he was going to do about the farm. Freeman couldn't blame his father for picking a bad time to discuss such matters. Spring was upon them, and Andy Yoder had plans to make. A schedule to keep, regardless of the flighty whims of Helen Schrock.

"We took on two extra fields on lease."

Yet another thing that they had talked about previously. "I—I'm sorry," Freeman said, finally finding his voice. "I can still figure something out. I can still come help."

His *dat* sat unmoving, his expression blank. Freeman couldn't tell whether he was angry, disappointed or merely stating the facts. That was his father. Emotions were best left to the side when it came to business. "That's gonna be hard to do if you're farming without a help-mate."

He opened his mouth to say with any luck he would have Evie by his side, but he stopped himself before saying anything. Several reasons factored in. One, Evie hadn't yet agreed to marry him. Two, they wouldn't be married by harvest even if she had. And three, Evie came with a set of limitations. Not that it mattered to him, but their workload split would be quite different than it would've been between him and Helen.

"What?" his *mamm* asked. She had sensed his hesitation.

"Are you sure Helen isn't coming back?" Claire asked.

"Claire!" This time Rebecca didn't temper her cry, and their sister's name came out in a full-on screech.

"Well," Claire said. "Obviously he's got something else to say."

Freeman cleared his throat. He hated keeping secrets, but it wasn't something he could tell yet. When he could, he was going to announce it to all the world. He could hardly wait. Until then, it had to stay locked inside. Until he convinced Evie that they were meant to be wed.

He turned back to his father. "It'll be hard, but we'll get it done."

Evie straightened and wiped the back of one forearm against her cheek.

Once again, she was in the barn helping Mattie milk the goats. Though "helping" was too generous a term, and Evie was beginning to feel a little guilty for using up so much of her sister's time. It seemed to take twice as long for Mattie to milk the goats with Evie as it did with Naomi. But if Evie was going to make this dream a reality she had to practice. She had to get her own rhythm down with the beasts.

"Maybe goats aren't your thing," Naomi said from the door.

Evie whirled around to glare at her sister. She wasn't the only one.

"That wasn't necessarily nice, Naomi," Mattie said with a stern look.

"I'm not trying to be mean," Naomi replied. She never was. But Naomi called 'em as she saw 'em, though sometimes her take on situations wasn't always kind.

"I've just got to get used to it," Evie defended. That was the plain and simple truth. She had milked animals before, the cow her father kept at the house among them. But she had never milked so many animals all at one time, and never when her livelihood and the opportunity for that sweet little house at the edge of town was at stake. "I won't have this many," she said, repeating her own thoughts.

"How many do you think you'll need?" Mattie asked.

Honestly, she had no idea. "I only need enough so I can make lotions and soaps."

Naomi crossed her arms and leaned back against the doorjamb of the barn. "So? How many is that?"

Mattie shot Naomi an exasperated look, then turned her attention to Evie. "We'll have to figure out how much milk you need each day to make the number of soaps and lotions that you need."

"How do we do that?" Evie asked, ignoring Naomi's grunt.

"Each goat is going to produce a certain amount of milk. It may vary, but you can estimate how much milk you will have from the number of goats you have and get it pretty close."

"Okay." With that information she would know how many goats she needed.

"First you need to know how much soap and lotion you'll need to generate enough money to make ends meet."

It made perfect sense. Evie should've thought of that herself. As much as she had been dreaming about her little house and having some goats and making lotions and soaps and having an independent life, somehow she let the pragmatic part of her dream slip past her.

"Here's a thought," Mattie added. "You keep helping me out here. Naomi can join us too." She shot their sister a look.

Naomi straightened but said nothing.

"In the meantime," Mattie continued, "you can start making lotions and soaps. That way you can gauge how much the ingredients cost, how much product each produces and how much you can charge for each one."

She definitely should've thought of this, but truthfully, she had been caught up in the physicality of actually milking the goats to consider the financial bearing. That was Mattie, always pragmatic. If anyone knew how to make a business run, it was Mattie Ebersol Byler.

"That's a good idea, sister," Evie said. "I'll start collecting the things I need to make lotions and soaps, and I'll keep helping you out here, as long as I'm not in your way." The idea was pure excitement, making her nearly breathless with anticipation. As she was building her dream into a reality, Freeman was working through his own.

What breath she had left caught in her throat as his name skittered across her thoughts. He had proposed. To her. It was something she had wanted her entire life but never dared dream of. And even then she couldn't have it.

"You could never be in my way." Mattie said with a smile. Her words pulled Evie from her suddenly sad musings. "Just think—with three of us milking the goats, it'll take no time at all."

She might not have Freeman, but she had her sisters. What more could a girl ask for?

Chapter Four

After all the talk about milking goats and making soaps and how many goats would be needed, Evie still felt as if the ground beneath her was rocky. Or maybe it was shaky. That was why the following day she decided to meet the owner of the little house she'd planned to rent and talk to her once again to make sure she had all of her statistics right. Plus, it wouldn't hurt to let her know that she was still interested in that property.

"Where are you headed?" Mattie asked as she watched Evie hook up the horse to the carriage. Evie had learned long ago if she didn't want everyone to know she was leaving and going somewhere, her best course of action was to hook the carriage up while it was still in the outbuilding and allow the horse to pull it out for her. She had almost gotten away with it this time. Except Mattie had come out onto the porch to sweep the dead leaves and such from the boards.

Evie held the horse's reins in one hand and waved the other one, still attached to her crutch. It flipped in the air like a dead fish. "Oh, you know. To the fabric store."

Great. Now she would have to stop by the fabric store, so she didn't tell her sister a lie.

Please don't ask to go too. Please don't ask to go too. Please don't ask to go too. Evie held her breath.

Mattie gave a small nod. "Okay, be careful."

Evie did her best not to let her relief show on her face, or in the sag of her shoulders. She'd been holding herself stiff as she waited for Mattie to answer. She wasn't going to the fabric store. She was going into town—specifically to the edge of town—to the little white clapboard house that she had had her eye on.

The house that was going to make her independent, with her little goat farm. A haven where she made lotions and soaps to sell and supported herself, and where everything was going to be sunshine and roses. Because that was what she wanted.

"Okay, thanks," Evie said, leading the horse and buggy out of the barn. As she said the words she heard a rattle toward the road. She paid it no mind and was pulling herself up into the carriage when another yellow buggy turned down the driveway. Someone was coming to visit.

Evie grabbed the blanket behind the seat and covered her legs with it. Her legs didn't have the best circulation when she was sitting, and it was always good to cover them to keep them warm.

"Where you off to?"

Evie looked up as Freeman slung himself down from his carriage.

She rarely had visitors, and when she did it was either Freeman or Helen. She could only imagine what Freeman needed today.

"I'm going to the fabric store," she said, that lie coming out again. Well, she supposed now that she actually planned to stop by the fabric store, it wasn't really a lie. She just left out the part about going to visit her cute little house.

Freeman nodded. "Well, can I ride along?"

Evie's jaw dropped open. "To the fabric store? You want to go to the fabric store with me?"

"Well, I—no, not really. I thought we might talk a bit, and if you're going to the fabric store and I ride along..."

Time was slipping away, and now that she had to make an extra stop at the fabric store, Evie had none to waste. She bit back a sigh and nodded her head toward the space beside her. "Get in."

He swung up next to her in the buggy. She gave her sister a quick wave goodbye.

"Okay," she said, as they got to the end of the drive. "I'm not really going to the fabric store. I mean, I'm going to the fabric store, but I've got another errand to run too. Are you sure you want to go?"

"Jah," he said. "I'm sure."

Evie would have much preferred it if he had gotten out of the buggy and let her take care of this business alone. And it had nothing to do with his rugged form sitting next to her on the small bench. Or the warmth from him that seeped into her very being. It was too comfortable having him sit close like that. It made her have ideas that she shouldn't have, ideas about getting married one day and having a baby of her own. Those ideas and dreams that she had squashed a long time ago.

"Where else are you going?" he asked.

Evie was reluctant to say, but she had told enough lies for the day. "There's this house at the edge of town. A Mennonite woman owns it. She lost her husband not too long ago. Anyway, it's got a little guesthouse in the back with a little bit of land. Not very big, but perfect for one person."

He turned to look at her and leaned back, in apparent surprise that registered on his handsome face. "Are you saying what I think you're saying?"

"What?" she asked, hating that her voice sounded so defensive. She had known she would get pushback from her family and friends when she decided to move out on her own. She was already prepared for it. "I can't live by myself?"

He shook his head. "I didn't say that. Who said that?"

"It doesn't matter," she replied. So, no one had actually *said* it to her, but she could tell that Naomi was thinking it. Mattie also seemed concerned that she wanted to gain this independence. But Evie had to. She had to prove to herself that she could do it.

"A place of your own though," he said with another small shake of his head. "That's a lot of responsibility."

Jah, something that she had been learning daily as she tried to milk goats that didn't want to be milked. At least not by her.

"Are you saying I can't do it?" Again, there was that defensive edge to her voice, but she did have something to prove, and she was going to prove it.

"I'm not saying that at all, but you do have certain limitations, Evie. Limitations that you should take into account. What happens if you were to fall?"

"I'm not going to fall."

"I'm sure David said the same thing."

David Byler was Mattie's first husband, and the father of her children. He'd had some sort of spell and fallen into the manure pit. It had been deep enough down, and he hit his head wrong and broke his neck. And that was that. Evie knew that he had no intentions of falling, but she couldn't live her life around fear of accidents.

"That's not fair. He had some sort of issue with his vision. I'm sure he just stepped wrong."

"And the same thing could happen to you."

"None of us know what's going to happen, and I need to do this. You're my friend," she said. "Why are you trying to talk me out of this?"

"Because I am your friend." He glared at her.

Evie glared back, then hated the fact that she had to turn around and look at the road to see where she was driving. She hated having to back down to his accusatory stare. "What a friend should do is support another friend."

"Who acted like I shouldn't buy the farm yesterday?"

"That's different. I just don't want you to go around feeling that Helen's going to come home any minute and that things will go right back to the way they were."

She hated the words once they slipped from her lips. She wasn't supposed to say that to him. She *was* supposed to be supportive.

"It seems you're the only one that thinks that. I've already made my peace with it. That's my farm, not Helen's."

"I know it's important for you to have something of your own. Something that no one can take away." She could almost see the wheels of his thoughts turning. Could almost tell the moment when he realized that he would have to answer, and the answer was in her favor.

"Jah," he said reluctantly. "It's important."

"It's the same for me." The words were almost a whisper.

He jerked his gaze to hers, understanding lighting his brown eyes.

"Just one thing," she said, glancing away and biting her lip, hoping he would accept these terms.

"What's that?"

"You can't tell my family. Please. Not yet. I kind of hinted to the idea, but I don't want Dat to know yet."

"What about Naomi and Mattie?"

"They know." Even if Naomi didn't approve.

"What do they think?"

There was something in his tone. Something that seemed to say he doubted her ability. Why did everyone have to be against her? Her whole life she had felt as if she were swimming upstream, going against the current. Everything was hard. Everything was like wading through peanut butter, physically and emotionally. She wished things would go smoothly. Maybe even easily. If only for a time or two, but she supposed that wasn't in God's plan for her. She'd had to work hard for everything she had, from learning to walk to being able to care for herself. This was the next step in her progression.

"About like you, I guess. They say they're supportive and yet they try to talk me out of it every chance they get."

Freeman had the audacity to look hurt. "I did not try to talk you out of it."

"What do you call it then?"

"Posing questions to you, trying to figure out if this is what you really want."

"Why would you do that?" She pinned him with another stare even as she slowed the buggy toward the upcoming driveway.

"I don't know," he said, shifting uncomfortably in the power of her glare.

"This is it," Evie said, but she wasn't about to let the subject drop. She pulled the buggy into the driveway next to the plain blue sedan already parked there. Then she set the brake and turned to face Freeman. "I'll tell you why. Because you're worried. Because you love me. Because you're my friend. I hear the same thing from them, and I understand. But what you're doing is undermining my confidence. And, well… I don't like that."

He drew back, she was certain in surprise. It wasn't often she stood up for herself. Okay, never. But today was different. What was that *Englisch* saying? *Today is the first day of the rest of your life.* That was how she felt. Today was the first day of the rest of her life, and she was going to live it the way she wanted to live it. As a goat farmer in a cottage at the edge of Millers Creek.

She held his gaze for what seemed like an eternity, only breaking that connection when she heard Judy call her name.

"Evie." A woman in a dress much like her

own came bustling out of the house. Her covering was dark, and her dress had a small print on it, but other than that and the car parked in the driveway, a person might believe they were of the same religion. Of course, Evie could tell all the small differences that someone who wasn't a part of the Plain lifestyle couldn't determine, but she had realized long ago outsiders could hardly tell a difference at all.

"Hi, Judy," Evie called, somehow injecting cheer into her voice so Judy would think everything was fine. "This is my friend Freeman. He wanted to look at the house today too."

Judy raised her brows high over her wire-rimmed glasses. "Oh."

"It's not—" Evie started then bit off the words. What good would it do to explain to everyone that she and Freeman were only friends? She had already told Judy that the house would be a single occupancy. If she hadn't told her differently, why would the woman think there was a change?

Judy waited patiently as Evie gingerly climbed down from the buggy. Once again, she could tell Freeman was hovering and wanted to help, but Evie had groomed a hard-won independence, and she wasn't about to let it go now, especially not just because her friend was impatient.

"I wanted to come and look at the house again and tell you that I'm still interested. I do want it," Evie said as she drew nearer to Judy.

Thankfully Freeman had fallen behind her, still hovering, but somehow comforting now in his presence. This was a big step for Evie, and she was glad to be sharing it with him.

"Come on then," Judy said, motioning for them to follow. She led them down the concrete walk that wound around the edge of the house to the large field behind. That was another thing that Evie was grateful for. There was a wide sidewalk that connected the driveway and the guesthouse where she would be living. She could maneuver it easily on her crutches, and it kept her out of the mud and snow when wintertime came. Another sign that this was the perfect house for her.

Not much had changed since she had been there the last time. The same green shade covered the windows, the same small dining room table sat next to the kitchen. Other than that, there was no furniture, save an end table that had been left in the living room along with a kerosene lamp that had been placed on top.

"Do you have furniture?" Freeman asked.

"Do you?" She eyed him innocently.

He sputtered. "Claire and Rebecca are supposed to be helping me find some things. I don't need much to start off."

Evie sniffed. "Neither do I." She had her bed from her *dat*'s, and she was certain she could find a chair or two somewhere. The dining room table set came with the place, and the kitchen was fully equipped with a propane refrigerator and a gas stove. What more could she need? Except for goats.

"I'm glad you're still interested," Judy said. "I was worried about leasing it out and having someone untrustworthy move in."

Evie could see where that would be a big concern for a widow. Perhaps that was why Judy was so willing to allow her time to get the money together.

"I'm not sure when I'll be able to move in," she said. She still had a lot of experiments to run. "It might be a couple months, maybe even June."

Judy blinked, then nodded. "Okay. That's okay, I guess."

It wasn't, Evie could tell.

She hated that she was failing in this part of her plan to move out. She still had to figure out how to milk the goats and how to make goat milk soaps and all the other little parts so that she could afford to live on her own. She was certain that if she ran short of money her father would help, but that was not what she wanted from her life. She wanted independence.

"Let me give you a deposit." Evie pulled her purse off her wrist and started taking cash out. "I have a couple of hundred dollars here?" She hadn't meant to sound so unsure.

Judy held out one hand to stay her offering and shook her head. "No. That's all right. You don't have to do that. I will save it for you."

"If you save it for me, you're not making any money on it, and I don't want you to be strapped."

Judy smiled sweetly. "I don't want you paying for a place that you are not living in. I'll keep it for you for another month or two. How's that? Then we can go from there."

Evie almost wilted with relief. "That sounds perfect."

"Evie…" Freeman started as they headed for home. He had been patient, as she had perused the bolts at the fabric store.

He knew she loved to sew, and he had listened as she chatted about her plan to make the girls matching dresses. She was even contemplating making one for Mattie too. Especially since her goat Charlie had taken to nibbling on things she oughtn't. When she was bored or ignored, or both.

"Jah?" she prodded when he seemed stalled in whatever it was he was about to say. She gave him a small glance, then looked back to the road ahead. They were almost back to Mattie's house.

"How are you going to pay for that house? I mean, that's the goal, right? Move in and work and live on your own, *jah?"*

"Jah." She paused for a moment, seemingly reluctant to tell him her plans. "I'm going to raise goats."

"What? Goats?" He stared at her as if she had lost her mind. Maybe she had.

"I'm going to get a small herd and put them behind the house—I've already talked to Judy about having livestock—and I'm going to milk them. Then I'm going to make lotions and soaps with the milk and sell them here locally."

A lot of stores took locally made products on consignment from crafters. Everything from Amish-made faceless dolls to jams and jellies, candies and canned goods. Everyone knew that Tottie Yoder made a fine living growing the special cucumbers they used for their white "church pickles."

That wasn't the problem.

"Have you actually tried to milk a goat?" Freeman asked.

"Jah." But she didn't seem quite sure. Definitely not sure enough to own a herd and depend on them for her living.

"Goats are terrible. I mean, you'd be better off trying to milk cows. They aren't so…ill-behaved."

Evie stiffened, and despite her strict posture, he could hear the desperation and anxiety in her voice. "I'll admit that goats can be ornery." That was putting it mildly. "But who ever heard of cow's milk lotion and soap?"

He wasn't sure what made goat's milk so special that people needed to include it in their personal care products, but he wasn't about to question that now.

"Why does any milk need to be involved? Isn't making the lotion and soap chore enough?"

She shook her head, eyes still straight ahead. "I want it to be special."

"Evie—" Freeman started, though he wasn't sure exactly how to finish.

Well, he knew, but could he say it? Could he convince her?

She glanced at him out of the corner of her eye. "What is it?" She seemed almost wary as she waited for him to continue.

"I have a solution to both our problems."

"I wasn't aware that you had a problem."

"Dat leased out two extra fields for this year's harvest," he explained. "He wanted me to help bring it in, but I told him yesterday that I would be working my own farm."

"I'm sure there will be plenty of hands when the time comes," she murmured as she pulled the buggy into the drive at her sister's house.

"But the solution is right there. Marry me, Evie. Marry me, and I'll help you with the goats. You can help me on my farm, and Dat will have me there to help when he needs it. And—"

He stopped as Evie raised one hand to quiet his words.

She closed her eyes, and he knew what was coming before she even spoke. Somehow he managed to keep a neutral expression on his face—at least he hoped it didn't show the pain he was feeling inside. That pain was confusing. This was Evie, his Evie. She would never break his heart. So why did it feel like it was breaking when she finally opened her eyes and said the words he'd been dreading to hear.

"No, Freeman. You know I can't marry you."

Chapter Five

"No? Why no?"

Evie shook her head, then shivered as her *kapp* strings tickled her neck. The girls in their district had recently started leaving theirs untied like the women in Lancaster, and she hadn't yet gotten used to the sensation of them floating freely around her neck. "I can't marry you." He would never know what it cost her to say those words.

"Evie, this has nothing to do with the promise."

"Really?" She set the brake and turned in the seat to look at him, suddenly wishing that she hadn't.

"Really. It's simply the perfect solution."

She pressed her lips together and glared at him. All the while she could almost feel her sisters watching from the house. Thankfully no one came out on the porch to see why they were still sitting in the buggy.

"I mean it. You and I can live on the farm. I'll help you with the goats, and you can help me by canning and taking the vegetables to the market, and life will be sweet."

Life will be sweet.

If only it could happen that way.

"What about my house?" That had been the entire reason for going to town today. She had this house all picked out. She had a plan. She was working toward her own independence, and he was trying to take it away from her.

Truly, there was a part of her—she was a romantic, after all—that would love nothing more than to fall into his dream. But if she did, what would she have proven to herself? She would never know if she could do it on her own.

All her life she'd had help. She'd had people helping her do this and that and the other. For once, just once, she wanted to know that she could do things by herself.

"It's a terrible solution," she finally managed.

How could she make him understand? She couldn't. She had learned long ago that no matter how hard they tried, a person could not fully understand what she had been through. So many had tried. Her beautiful family. Her wonderful friends. But even the others that she had met in the hospital who also suffered from spina bifida couldn't fully understand *her*. They couldn't comprehend *her* goals and *her* trials, her dreams and the limitations that kept her from succeeding. Because no matter how hard a person tried, no one could live a day in someone else's skin. There was no way to truly know what another person was feeling or going through, no matter how badly they wanted to.

"I care about you. You care about me. We could build a good life together," he said.

She didn't want to hear those words from him. She needed more than his caring. She wanted his love. But how could she ever know that he loved her for her and her alone and not because she represented saving grace to him?

Never in her wildest dreams had she ever imagined that he would propose to her—at least not again, and not seriously as an adult. Even more out there, she would have laughed if anyone had told her that she would be turning down Freeman Yoder's marriage proposal.

She didn't feel like laughing. She felt like crying. Why was life so hard?

"Why? I don't understand why." He eyed her as if he didn't really know her at all.

The urgency and caring she heard in his voice made her want to back up on her refusal, made her want to throw her arms around him and never let go. Take that chance. But she had to remain tough. Or she'd never get past this with her heart intact.

"I'm being practical," she told him. "One of us needs to be." She couldn't tell him the real reason. He could think that she was being childish and stubborn and mean and hateful, but she couldn't tell him that she loved him and was afraid that no matter what he said he still loved Helen. "The organic farm is your dream. Raising goats and making soaps and lotions is mine. Surely you can see that."

"There's no reason why the two of us can't merge our dreams."

"There's a hundred reasons. Helen promised to return to Millers Creek. What will she think if she comes home and finds the two of us engaged?"

He seemed to think about it for a second. "I don't know, and I'm not sure I care."

"Freeman!"

"What I mean is I can't concern myself with that now. Helen knew what she was doing when she walked away. She can't expect me to be waiting for her to come back."

"It's not even been a week!" Yet another reason she couldn't accept his proposal. It was too soon.

She may have loved him most of her life, but he was just coming off the breakup with Helen. He didn't need to jump feetfirst into a new relationship, even with someone he had known forever.

He shrugged. "I'm buying a farm. I'm living through the goals I've made. I need a wife."

She shook her head. "Maybe. One day, but it can't be me."

"Why do I get the feeling that you aren't telling me everything?"

"I have no idea." She slammed her gaze into his so he would understand that she was serious. Then maybe he would stop questioning everything she said. She couldn't marry him, and she wished he would just drop it.

"Fine," he said, turning away and climbing down from the buggy.

She supposed she must have wilted his determination with her steely glare, but most likely Freeman had simply tired of the back and forth and gave up. She was afraid that he wouldn't accept defeat graciously, and the subject would come up again. She hoped she was ready for it when it did.

"What are you doing here?" Evie stood at the door of Mattie's house, staring out at the porch where Freeman Yoder waited.

"Tonight's the party. The Spring into Spring Party."

"I know that," Evie said. "So why aren't you on your way there?"

He tilted his head to one side as if studying a particularly interesting thing that perhaps he had never seen. "We said we were going together."

Evie opened her mouth to say something. Then she closed it and shook her head. "That was when Helen was going too."

So often she ended up as the third wheel on dates, and for the most part she hated it, but at the same time she loved her two best friends. She didn't always love the relationship between them. Even though she knew that she and Freeman could never be a couple, she wasn't sure that Helen was the right one for him. In fact, there were times when she thought that Helen downright took advantage of Freeman, and that Freeman allowed it because it was easier that way. Evie didn't know. She was standing on the outside looking in. Where she always was.

"Why wouldn't we still go together now?"

"Because Helen's not here."

Freeman shook his head in apparent confusion. "That doesn't make any sense. We always go together."

He made it seem all so simple when it was anything but. Especially not after his marriage proposal from the day before. As far as she was concerned, that changed everything.

"I don't know, Freeman."

"What is wrong with you, Evie? Get your sweater and let's go."

Evie glanced behind her. Naomi stood there holding Charlie by the collar so the goat couldn't spring out onto the porch and bite Freeman's pant legs. Her sister was also listening intently to what they were saying.

Evie gritted her teeth and stepped outside, closing the door behind her. "You know why." She dropped her tone in further assurance that Naomi wouldn't be able to overhear.

He seemed to think about it for a moment, then he reared his head back, mouth open in an exclamation of *Oh, now I get it*. "You're talking about yesterday," Freeman said.

Evie stamped one of her crutches against the boards of the porch. "Of course I'm talking about yesterday." What was wrong with him? Was he being deliberately obtuse or was he just clueless?

"It's okay," he said. "Yesterday doesn't change anything. Not if you give me a chance."

"A chance for what?"

"To prove myself. You don't believe that I care for you. That we would make a fine couple. Many marriages have started with a lot less than what's between us."

She didn't want to give him a chance to prove anything. It would require her to be too strong. She wasn't sure she had the strength to resist Freeman when he turned on the charm. If he was trying to convince her that they needed to get married, he would be charming for sure.

"Are you chicken?" His tone was playful and his smile mischievous. But she knew what he was trying to do. And only her best friend could cajole her into a positive response. If she didn't go, she would never hear the end of it from him. So she had to give in. She had to go to the Spring into Spring Party with him tonight. Though not without conditions.

"As friends," she said, snagging his gaze and holding it firm. He needed to know she was serious. She had to have him in her life so she was going to have to see this through the best way she could.

He nodded.

"As friends," she repeated. "Say it."

He cleared his throat. "As friends."

She stared at him. "I promise, Evie, we are going as friends. Say that."

For a moment she thought he might refuse, then he sighed and repeated the words, his voice holding an exasperated note.

"Okay then," she finally said. "I'll get my sweater."

She should've held her ground, Evie thought as she drank a cup of strawberry lemonade and surveyed the people all milling around. It was a typical party for their buddy bunch, a group within their youth group of close friends who got together on a more regular basis. Their buddy bunch gathered almost every Thursday night for something or another, weather permitting, of course. Any excuse to talk, eat food and play games.

As she had known from the start, couples were already starting to pair up. The last thing she wanted was to be coupled up with Freeman.

Okay, so it wasn't the *last* thing she wanted. More the last thing she *needed*. She couldn't go getting her hopes up that there could be anything more between them. As it was, it was killing her to deny his promise, to downplay his marriage proposal and to act like none of it affected her at all. But she had been pretending not to care more for him than mere friendship for twenty years. Why should she quit now? He might have his doubts, and she might have a few from time to time, but Helen was a valley girl at heart. Lancaster's glitz and drama would only hold her for so long before she craved the steady clip-clop lifestyle of Millers Creek. Evie would surely hate for her best friend to return only to hear rumors that Evie was encroaching on her one-time fiancé. Regardless of what Freeman said about the matter, she knew that when Helen returned, she would want Freeman back. They had been engaged for so long, and they had been coupled up even longer than that. They had promised themselves to each other when they were mere teenagers. Barely old enough to understand what marriage even was. Feelings like that didn't go away overnight.

If he was going to insist that Helen wasn't returning, then Evie supposed the very least she should do was turn Freeman's attention somewhere else. Her plan was simple. Find someone else for him to date, feel the waters out and see if he would take Helen back or not. Give him options.

While she herself was not an option at all, the room was filled with eligible young ladies that he could date, and possibly even marry, on the off chance that Helen didn't return, or she returned and didn't want to marry him. At least then, when Helen returned, it wouldn't be Evie encroaching on her husband but someone else. Their friendship would be saved.

It would break her heart to see Freeman dating yet another woman, when she knew that she could not have him. It certainly beat losing her best friend over what would essentially turn out to be nothing.

Even as the couples started pairing up, there were a few girls clustered together, standing next to the dessert table, whispering among themselves and laughing behind their hands. Maybe one of them could provide Freeman with enough distraction that he would forget that sweet—er, silly, silly marriage proposal from the day before.

There was Esther Schrock—she was Helen's sister. She was standing next to Rebecca Yoder, Freeman's own sister, who was standing next to Harriet Raber. Harriet wasn't kin to Freeman or Helen, but she was definitely too tall. After all, if Evie was going to try to set him up with someone, then the girl needed to be a good match for him. What if they happened to fall in love and wanted to get married? It wouldn't do for them to be mismatched from the start, and Harriet was definitely a mismatch to Freeman. Then there was Tessie Peight. At twenty, she was too young. Out of the question.

Evie scanned the room once more, her gaze landing on Faith Ebersol, her own cousin. Try as she might, Evie couldn't find anything wrong with Faith except that she was her cousin.

Faith was pretty enough and sweet enough and short enough. Or not too tall. Or whatever it was so that Evie couldn't rule her out. Except that Evie didn't want Freeman dating Faith.

As she stood debating, Naomi sauntered up to Faith.

Naomi!

She would be a better choice. She would be—no, she wouldn't. Evie was only teasing herself. Naomi would eat poor Freeman alive. Nope, the better choice by far was Faith. Evie didn't know how her heart would feel having to watch the two of them court. Maybe she should hold out hope that Helen was coming back.

If not, she supposed she could try to set Freeman up with a girl from one of the Renno Amish districts in the valley, a black topper. Even that might not be far enough away to protect her heart.

"So, what do you think?"

Evie whirled around as her sister Sarah Ann glided up, pressing the palms of her hands down her black apron. "Is that a new dress?"

She had never seen her sister wear such a color of blue, deep and dark and mixed with green, so it looked like the pictures of the ocean she had seen on magazines at the checkout counter in the supermarket. It made Sarah Ann's eyes look even bluer than normal.

Sarah Ann bit her lip and nodded shyly. "I made it especially for tonight."

"Special…" Ugh. She had been so wrapped up in her own situation with Freeman, she had forgotten all about Mose and Sarah Ann. And Noah Peight. And Judah Peachy.

Double ugh! What a tangle.

No, this was good. She could concentrate on Mose and Sarah Ann tonight, then maybe she could think of someone better for Freeman to spend time with than Faith. *Jah*, it was a good plan.

"It's a beautiful dress," Evie finally said. "You look beautiful in it. I'm sure Mose is over there drooling in his punch."

Where was Mose?

She allowed her gaze to travel around the room again. Just like the girls who had clustered around the dessert table, the boys were grouped around the fireplace, each one tossing something in to simply watch it burn.

Unfortunately, he was standing right next to Freeman. Her friend caught her eye and grinned as if he knew she couldn't keep her attention away from him. Not good. Despite herself, Evie smiled back.

"What is he doing?" Sarah Ann asked. "I'm afraid to look."

"He's just standing there." Looking disinterested in everything, including Sarah Ann. Evie had started this, and she needed to see it through. Sarah Ann was counting on her.

"Has…has he been looking at me tonight?"

Evie didn't have an answer. Again, she was too wrapped up in her own issues and had completely forgotten about the Mose King situation with Sarah Ann. She could fix this though. Starting right now.

"Stay here," she said, turning so she could make her way across the room.

Sarah Ann reached out a hand and tugged on Evie's sleeve.

She stopped.

"Where are you going?" Sarah Ann asked.

"I'm going to make something happen," Evie said. "You just stay here and look beautiful."

"What?"

Evie ignored her sister and continued across the room to where the men were standing, huddled together as if they might catch something from the girls.

"Evie," Freeman warmly greeted. "Where have you been?"

That was when Evie realized that her plan to talk to Freeman in front of Mose about Sarah was probably not a good one. Because that meant she had to talk to Freeman, and she pretty much dismissed him at the beginning of the party. Now she was seeking him out. It didn't look good for her claims that they couldn't get married. Not that talking to someone was enough to constitute a wedding. But it sure made her look interested in him, when she wasn't. Interested in him. Well, in anything more than a friend.

She mentally shook her head at herself and resisted the urge to close her eyes as if she could blink and start everything over again. Instead, she smiled back at Freeman. She shouldn't be afraid to talk to him. That was ridiculous. He had been her best friend for years, and she should act as if everything was normal. Act as if he hadn't asked her to marry him. *Jah*, that was the ticket, as they say.

"Would you like something to drink?"

Evie shook her head. She had abandoned a half-full glass of strawberry lemonade to come over here and talk to him. With any luck she could execute her mission of Project Mose King and go back to her drink before it even got warm.

"I was just talking to Sarah Ann." Her voice was bright and a little too loud, but she needed to make sure that Mose overheard her. "She made her dress especially for tonight. Isn't it gorgeous?"

Freeman blinked at her; confusion had overtaken his expression. "*Jah*. I guess so."

If Evie had been sitting down, she would have smacked a hand to her forehead. At times like this she missed Helen most of all. Poor Freeman might be her best friend in other matters, but he surely didn't talk about dresses and recipes and all the other things that she talked about with Helen.

Even worse was the doubt that filled his voice. She wanted Mose to look at her sister with bright eyes, to notice how special she was. The tone of Freeman's voice did not induce special thinking.

"Hey," she said, this time lowering her voice where surely only Freeman could hear. It must've worked because he took a step closer to her in order to understand what she was saying. "Just say she looks beautiful, okay?"

"What?" Freeman said at a normal tone.

Evie shot him a look that she hoped said S*top being so dumb and listen to what I'm saying*, but she wasn't sure it came across the way she intended. "Just say she's beautiful. I'll explain later."

"On the ride home, we can talk?" These words were spoken even louder, and that was when she realized that Freeman might have his own agenda. He was putting his stamp on her, letting everyone at the party know that there might be something more than friendship between the two of them. Great.

"Please."

He smiled at her again, that twinkle back in his eyes. He really was handsome when he grinned like that. *"Jah,"* he said even louder than his comment about the ride home. "Sarah Ann does look lovely tonight."

Evie kept her voice as low as possible. "Mose King," she said with a pointed look in the young man's direction.

He was standing right behind Freeman and surely had heard every word that Freeman had said.

Still Freeman caught on and elbowed Mose

in the side to gain his attention. "Have you talked to Sarah Ann Ebersol tonight?"

Mose turned around, a perplexed look on his face. That expression seemed to be running rampant these days.

"Sarah Ann Ebersol?" Mose asked.

Evie inwardly cringed. He said her sister's name as if he'd never heard it before. She had been so certain that she had seen him glancing Sarah Ann's way at the last meeting they had. Well, even if she was wrong, Mose seemed to be unaffiliated with any girl in their group. Perhaps he wasn't set on dating anyone yet and Freeman talking up Sarah Ann might spark his interest. She hoped anyway. She didn't want her sister to be disappointed yet again. Because Judah Peachy was no Helen. Without a doubt, he was never coming back to Millers Creek.

Chapter Six

❦

Once Freeman got her alone, he was definitely going to find out what she was up to.

After she had talked so loudly about her sister Sarah Ann in front of Mose King, like she wanted him to overhear, she had begged off saying she needed a bit of fresh air. He had offered to go with her, but she had declined and moved quickly away.

Now he watched from across the room while Evie sat in a chair on the other side watching everyone else. She looked so pretty sitting there with her bright hazel eyes and sweet, sweet smile. So pretty. And so lonely. It was a shame how she seemed to linger on the fringes. Why had he never noticed it before? Yet seeing it and understanding it tonight made him realize she was always there, just outside of the circle. He didn't like it. Not at all.

There had to be something he could do to get her more involved. No wonder she felt like an outsider. However, if he went over to talk to her, what good would that do? It would only be the two of them talking. They could do that on the way home. No, he wanted to see her out and doing things with more people. Not just with him. She was a valuable member of their community, and he wanted her to know it. His heart ached that she didn't.

Someone had pushed all the tables back to the walls and left the middle of the floor open. Now, they were playing some dumb party game that looked like human tic-tac-toe—girls against the boys.

Evie could join in that, he supposed. It wasn't like she had to be fast or nimble. He could understand if there was a softball game or something like that, but instead, she was still on the fringes.

Somehow, he got the awful feeling that no matter what they were doing she would always be on the periphery, as if she were punishing herself for not being like everyone else. Suddenly he was swamped with the memory of that day in the first grade when he asked her to marry him. He had remembered feeling so sad as she was sitting there all by herself. He wanted to be her friend, so she didn't have to be alone. Now here they were twenty years later.

They were friends, and she was still alone. It didn't make any sense.

Apparently, there was more to be done than just "be friends." He was going to do something about it right now.

She smiled sweetly at him, a smile that nearly made his heart stop. She had such a great smile. It was the smile of his best friend, and he knew how lucky he was to have her.

"What are you doing over here all alone?" His voice hitched on the last word.

"Watching." She shrugged, her hands still on her crutches, legs out in front.

"Why aren't you playing?"

She shook her head. "I think they're making up the rules as they go along."

He glanced over to where the others were playing. After watching the game for a bit, he looked back to Evie, who was observing their antics with a smile on her face.

He had practically had to drag her to the party so he didn't have to come alone. She came, however reluctantly—but she was there and for that he was grateful. He supposed he would eventually get used to going places without Helen and used to the sad looks everyone gave him. He would get used to not being part of a couple, but until then, Evie had helped him save face.

"Thank you," he murmured, reaching down and touching her shoulder before he could think better of it. He eased his hand back, immediately missing her warmth.

If she thought the action was strange, her face didn't show it. Neither did her words. "What are you thanking me for?"

"For coming with me tonight."

"As friends," she reminded him.

He nodded. "As friends." He could be patient. He had time to show her how perfect they were for each other and how good their life together could be. The thought of Evie not being his partner on the farm, in his life, suddenly made his heart ache.

"Have you talked to Faith tonight?"

Her question jarred him out of his reverie. "Faith? Your cousin Faith?"

"That would be the one."

"No. Why?"

The smile on Evie's face turned a bit dreamy and he wondered what she was thinking about. "I don't know. I thought you might want to talk to her."

What was she up to now? "Okay, I'll bite. Why?"

Evie shook her head. "You got this all wrong. I'm just asking."

"Uh-huh." Freeman eyed her in disbelief.

"I mean, you think she's pretty, right?"

There wasn't a person in the building who would say that Faith Ebersol wasn't pretty. She had porcelain skin, ebony hair and the brightest blue eyes he'd ever seen. Though he had to admit the descriptions came from Rebecca. It wasn't like he was poetic. Not like girls seemed to be. Still, the truth was that Faith Ebersol was a beautiful girl. Twenty-three and starting to settle in and find herself with hopes that her husband would soon find her.

"Jah," he said, trying not to sound overly enthusiastic about it. He didn't want Evie to get the wrong idea. Faith was beautiful, but that didn't mean he wanted to date her. It was a fact that Evie seemed to be missing. Because why else would she be talking to him about her cousin unless she was scoping out someone new for him?

He didn't want anyone new. He wanted Evie. It was as simple as that.

"She works hard too," Evie added. "Faith. You know, at the fabric store. She is a great seamstress."

"Better than you?"

Evie looked taken aback. "How do you know I sew?"

Freeman gave her a mysterious smile. "Everyone knows that you sew. And you're very good at it." He didn't need to tell her that Rebecca and Claire talked often about how clever Evie was with the sewing machine. Let her wonder about it a while, stew in it.

Evie sniffed. "Well, she's a very good seamstress all the same."

Freeman bit back a chuckle.

"She's also very good at crochet and knitting."

"I see. So, you're not any good at that?"

Evie shot him a frown. "Of course, I can crochet and knit. But we're not talking about me, we're talking about Faith."

"Oh, I'm aware," Freeman said.

"I know for a fact she made that shawl she's wearing."

"I know for a fact she's wearing a shawl because she's always cold."

Evie drew back and gave him another perplexed look. He was beginning to get used to her eyebrows crashing over the bridge of her nose. "How do you know that?"

He dipped his head to one side and made his expression as innocent as possible. "You just pick these things up, I guess." *When your sisters chatter nonstop at the dinner table.*

"Well, the good part of it is you wouldn't be cold in the wintertime," Evie continued.

"Why would that be?" Somehow Freeman had lost the point of this whole conversation, if it even had one.

"I'm just saying, when you start to date a person, you need to look at the talents and skills they can bring into a marriage."

"So, you're saying her skill as a yarn worker is something I should consider when I start looking for someone new to date?"

Evie's brows raised and her face got an animated look. Though he couldn't help but notice the excitement didn't quite reach her pretty eyes. "*Jah*, that's it. Since Faith is very good at crochet and knitting, your family would always have scarves and mittens and hats."

"Wouldn't we need coats too?"

Evie's excitement immediately fell. "You should be more serious about this. I thought you were looking for a wife."

"I asked you to marry me," he pointed out. The idea was becoming increasingly comfortable. Marrying Evie Ebersol.

"Freeman, be serious."

"I was," he said. "But I suppose that, if I get

cold before you agree to marry me, I'll just have to pay someone to knit me mittens, hats and scarves."

"You could have taken Faith home tonight if you wanted to," Evie said as she and Freeman started for her house. "I would've understood, you know. I could've ridden with Naomi." All of it was true, but Freeman looked at her like she was a complete stranger.

The man could be stubborn. She would give him that. Yet the same thing could be said about her. He thought he was being sweet, promising to marry her and uphold that long-ago promise, that silly promise no one expected him to honor. That she would never accept.

"No," he said, barely casting a glance in her direction before switching his attention back to the dark road ahead. "This suits me just fine. Right down to my shoes."

That didn't sound like stubbornness. That sounded like miscommunication. Perhaps she should have ridden home with Naomi anyway to show Freeman there was no hope in her ever marrying him.

Hope was such a strong word, so definite. He didn't need hope. He needed to recognize the truth—that he only wanted to marry her to save face. They had been friends for so long, companions, cohorts. Everyone knew they could get along like a house on fire. It would be no big jump for the two of them to get married—it certainly would not be viewed as a rebound romance like it would be if he married someone like Faith.

Then there was that stupid promise. The sweetest promise of her life, but it didn't matter. It didn't matter how sweet it was, how heartfelt it was, how out of character for a little Amish boy to propose to a girl he barely knew. None of that mattered because in the end, it was only words. As sweet as those words were, they meant nothing because he couldn't promise that.

Besides, twenty-two had come and gone. It was never coming back again. The promise was already broken. Not that she held him to it. He had made the promise to lift her spirits, and it had carried her through many tough years. Because of that promise, he had become her best friend. She couldn't give that up. Wouldn't give it up for the world.

"Why would I want to take Faith home?"

"Well, she's pretty, for one."

He'd caught her off guard. She had been trying to sing Faith's praises all night. Although

Faith was a lovely person, a wonderful cousin and so worthy of a good and godly husband, Evie was having trouble outlining all her good qualities to Freeman.

"I think we established that a while back," Freeman said. He flicked the reins over the horse's back and shot her a sideways look. A look that clearly said *I know what you're up to.*

"Listen," she said, surprising herself with the seriousness of the one word. All the playfulness was gone from her tone. "If you really do want a wife to help you with the farm… Faith is the perfect choice." It was so very hard for her to say those words. They nearly stuck in her throat, choking her with their validity. Somehow, she managed to say them, and she was thankful for that. Because otherwise Freeman was never going to get off this promise by himself. He didn't really want to marry her. He just thought he did, and until she got him distracted by something else, he was going to continue to deceive himself into believing that he did want to marry her.

Jah. This was the only way. She bit back the bitter taste of the kind words and started once more. "Faith is a good cook. Makes the tiniest stitches when she quilts, and she would be such a good mother." It was all the truth, but the words were nearly impossible to say. Evie was a little surprised that she managed to get them out without so much as a cough.

She didn't want Freeman to marry Faith. When it got down to it, she hadn't wanted Freeman to marry Helen. The hardest thing of all was knowing that she herself could never marry him. Despite his kind proposal. He was only trying to save face. He needed an able-bodied wife, and she needed her best friend.

Standing on the fringes, she watched a lot. She saw things, and she was able to help people. Like tonight when she was talking to Mose about Sarah Ann. A little nudge to help them along. To help Mose realize that Sarah Ann might be the one for him, and for Sarah Ann to accept that Judah Peachy was never coming back. *Jah*, this had to be God's plan for her. Evie was there to fix it all for those around her. Her own happiness would be found in the joy of others finding their happiness. It might not be fair, but what in life truly was?

Chapter Seven

"This must be it."

Freeman turned to the spot of fence where Samuel Byler was pointing. "Are you sure?"

The pair had been out walking the fence that enclosed Mattie's goat pen. Apparently, a few of the beasts had gotten out in the night—a feat only realized when they came walking up the driveway—and Samuel had come over to repair it.

"It doesn't look quite big enough for a goat to get through," Freeman added.

"Goats can be wily," Samuel said. "I learned that lesson the hard way."

He started dropping his tools on the ground next to their workspace.

Still Freeman wasn't convinced. He bent down to get a better look at the hole between the wires.

"Are you sure they can even get their head out of that?"

Samuel chuckled. "You know what they say, right? If the fence can hold water, it'll hold goats."

Freeman screwed up his face and tried to work that one out. "I had no idea they said that at all."

"*Jah*, well, every goat farmer knows the adage, that's for sure. I've fixed smaller spaces than this where goats were escaping. I don't know how they do it, but they do it."

Freeman eyed the gap once more and then nodded slowly. "I guess I'll have to take your word for it."

If goats were that clever, how in the world was Evie going to keep on top of them at her place? Not that she wasn't smart, but there was smart and there was physically being able to keep up. Which was why he worried about her so. Surely, she could understand that. But each time he asked, she seemed to get more and more offended. Was it wrong that he wanted to protect her? Help her? Be with her?

Freeman held the fence post as Samuel took out the clippers. "Would it be better to simply patch the hole?" *Maybe tightened up a bit?* he finished in his thoughts. Mainly because Samuel was already shaking his head.

"That might work with some goats, but not

this herd. Once a spot has been compromised it seems like it's all downhill from there. I found that the best thing to do is cut out the section, replace it and then go on."

"You're the boss, hoss," Freeman said.

Samuel chuckled and shook his head. "Hand me the pliers."

Freeman grabbed the tool and handed it over to Samuel, his thoughts slipping easily from fences back to Evie. "How did you know you wanted to marry Mattie?"

Samuel knelt on the ground and started measuring out the fencing. "I made a promise to my brother."

"David?"

"*Jah*. I promised him that if anything ever happened to him, I would take care of his family, and he promised the same to me," he continued. "It just so happened that I had to keep mine." His voice cracked a bit on the last word.

Freeman was stunned into silence. It was perhaps the last thing he had expected Samuel to say.

"So, I came back and fell in love with her."

"And it all worked out," Freeman said, his voice soft.

"*Jah.*" Samuel nodded but continued with his work.

"I—uh… I made a promise to Evie too," Freeman finally said. "When we were six years old, I promised her that if we weren't both married by the time we were twenty-two that I would marry her."

"Six, huh?"

"Jah," Freeman said. "Now here we are both twenty-six, neither one of us is married, and she won't give me the time of day. How'd you get Mattie to accept your promise?"

Samuel chuckled softly. "I'm not sure that's quite the same."

"I disagree. A promise is a promise, and we're both dealing with stubborn Ebersol women."

Samuel shrugged. "I suppose you're right about that. But it's about more than promises."

"So how did you do it?" Freeman pressed.

"It took some doing," Samuel explained. Freeman supposed that was downplaying the truth. Mattie had been pregnant, widowed for less than six months, and Samuel had just come back from years in the *Englisch* world. *Some doing* had to be an understatement.

"What about Helen? I thought you and Helen were getting married. Hold this." He gestured toward the new section of fence he was putting up over the old section he had yet to cut away.

"Are you going to cut out the bad part first?"

Samuel chuckled. "You have a lot to learn about goats."

Freeman shook his head. He supposed once he wore Evie down and got her to marry him, if she still wanted to make her goat milk lotions and soaps he would have to learn a bit about them. "What's that?"

"You can't give them an inch, or they'll take four miles."

"Which means?" Freeman asked.

"As soon as I cut away this piece of fence the goats will come running over here wherever they are and run out. Then we're in a world of hurt. So, we put the new fence up over the old fence and then cut the old fence away and—"

Freeman held up his hand to cut short Samuel's explanation. "Got it. Never underestimate the power of the goat."

"Now you're learning." Samuel smiled and wiped the sweat from his forehead with the sleeve of his shirt. "Now, Helen?"

"Helen's not coming back."

He pretty much settled himself to the fact. The first three days had been hard, *jah*, but he was dealing with it in his own way.

It was amazing how much clearer he could see now that she was not around. He didn't have much in common with her. They didn't share the same dreams. Not really. Sure, she talked some about organic farms, but she wasn't as excited about them as she was about the buttons she had bought at the dry goods store the day before. Then there was Evie, and Helen seemed to fall away to the background. How was that even possible?

"Even if she did, I can't imagine she'd stay for long, or even be happy living Amish here in the valley."

Samuel jerked his gaze to Freeman's. "You think she'll go Mennonite?"

"I honestly don't know. If I had to guess, I would say she's going to stay in Lancaster and live out her days with solar power and gray buggies."

Strangely enough, he was okay with that.

"Really?" Samuel seemed unconvinced.

"I'm pretty sure," Freeman countered. "Even if she does come back, even if she decides to stay here and remain Amish, it doesn't mean she's still going to want to marry me. She broke up with me before she left for Lancaster, remember?"

Samuel nodded. "I remember."

Then he should realize how unlikely it was that the two of them would ever marry, which brought him right back to Evie. "So how do I get Evie to see how wonderful our life together could be? How did you get Mattie to?"

"Hand me that box of U-shaped nails."

Freeman handed him the nails and stood back, holding the wiring in place while Samuel nailed it to the post.

Samuel gestured with one glove-covered hand. "Honestly, I have no idea how I got her to change her mind. In fact, I was about to go back to New Wilmington. I figured I couldn't be in love with her and stay in this community and watch her fall in love with someone else." He trailed off, shaking his head at the thought.

"I feel the same," Freeman said, only then realizing it. He loved Evie Ebersol. The feeling was sort of like being kicked by a mule. He had always loved that Evie was sweet and kind, but this was different. This was love. Love-love. The thought was both exciting and terrifying all in the same moment.

"I think you should hold off on whatever it is you're thinking about doing," Samuel said.

Freeman hadn't meant to be that transparent.

"If you start up with Evie now, everyone's going to think you're on the rebound from Helen."

"I've cared about Evie most of my life. How can that be a rebound?"

"I'm just telling it how I see it," Samuel said.

Freeman nodded slowly. *Jah*, he supposed to some it might seem that way. But at the end of the day, he knew the truth.

"I think she's in here," Mattie said as she opened the front door, pushing Charlie to one side to keep the goat from escaping.

Evie looked up from her crochet as Sarah Ann stepped into the house. Behind her, Mattie shut the door, quickly and efficiently trapping Charlie on the inside while she remained on the porch.

"Not quite finished out here," Mattie hollered through the closed door.

"Okay," Evie called back.

Charlie headbutted Sarah Ann on the leg until she bent down and scratched her on the top of the head. Charlie bleated with pleasure, then in complaint as Sarah Ann straightened and pinned her attention on Evie.

"So," Sarah Ann started, leaning back against the front door, Charlie still trying to gain her attention. "How do you think it went?"

"Come sit down," Evie said, nodding toward the couch.

She was stalling for time, but Sarah Ann didn't know that. Last night at the party she was supposed to have been helping her sister gain the attention of one Mose King. Yet all it seemed she did was worry about her own relationship with Freeman. Not that there was really a relationship, other than friendship. But with his insistence on making sure that she knew he meant to keep his promise to marry her and her insistence that regardless of his insistence she was not going to marry him, she had barely gotten around to working on the Mose–Sarah Ann situation.

"Now, these things take time," Evie said, eyeing her sister over her crochet. *Especially when the person who is trying to help you make a match is too busy trying to fend off the unappreciated advances of her best friend.*

"I know that," Sarah Ann said. "I...wanted an update. Do you think he looked at me? Do you think he noticed me?"

"Of course he noticed you. I think he might be interested. It's hard to say this early, you know."

Sarah Ann nodded. "I know. These things take time. I thought at least, maybe, he would ask to take me home from the party."

Evie shook her head. "That's a big step. Remember he didn't take anyone else home. So that's a good sign."

Color had risen high into Sarah Ann's cheeks, and Evie took a minute to note how pretty and young her sister looked sitting there, picking at a spot on her apron, biting her lip and worrying over true love. "I suppose," Sarah Ann said.

"And Noah?" Evie asked.

"I avoided him all night. I know. I'm a coward. I don't want to hurt his feelings, and I've tried to put it out there that I'm not up for dating him right now. But that would hurt his feelings, so I said that I'm not up for dating."

Evie shook her head. "That's going to ruin your chances with Mose if it gets around to him."

"I know," Sarah Ann cried. "What am I supposed to do?"

If only Evie had the answers.

It seemed that everyone always came to her when they had a problem, and in the past Evie always seemed to have a solution. But now… she was as stumped as everyone else.

"When's the next get-together?" Evie asked.

Sarah Ann gave a small shrug. "I don't know. Probably Thursday."

"What about the singing on Sunday?" Evie asked.

"I'd forgotten about that." Sarah Ann's voice held a miserable note.

Evie's heart went out to her sister. "Okay," Evie said, dropping her crochet into her lap and giving her sister her full attention. "Here's what we're going to do. You ride with me to the singing. Then I'll work on trying to get Mose to take you home that night. He might be bashful." She hoped anyway. She was certain she had seen Mose staring longingly at her sister, but she might have misinterpreted some of the situation. She did need to wear her glasses more, especially when she needed to see at a distance.

"You think it'll work?"

Truly, Evie didn't know what to think anymore, but she had promised her sister, and she would try to help in any way she could. "Of course." She said the two words with more conviction than she had ever shown anything in her life.

Thankfully Sarah Ann looked convinced. For that Evie was very grateful.

"What about you and Freeman?" Sarah Ann asked.

Evie shook her head. "We're just friends. It's always been that way."

Sarah Ann screwed up her face with doubt. "Somebody better tell him that."

"What do you mean?" Evie asked. She wasn't sure she could hold Sarah Ann's gaze, so she picked up her crochet and started once more working through the granny squares for the twins' blankets.

"Nothing bad. Just the way he looks at you."

"How's that?" Evie asked. She wanted to know and yet she didn't want to know. Because regardless of how he looked at her, nothing could ever come of it.

"All wistful like, you know? Like that feeling on your birthday when you expect someone to come by and say hi to you and they don't. That feeling you get in your stomach when that happens."

Evie nodded. She'd experienced that too many times to count, really. Times when she had wanted Freeman to stop by and say something and he came with Helen. Oh, she loved Helen, but it wasn't the same when they came as a couple.

"He looks at you like that."

Evie scoffed, even as her heart beat a little faster in her chest. He did? Could she believe it? Did she believe it? If it was true, how come she had never noticed?

She looked up from her crochet to find Sarah Ann studying her intently. "What?" she asked.

"There are none so blind," Sarah Ann started, but trailed off before finishing the adage. None so blind as those who will not see. That wasn't Evie. Not at all.

"There can't be anything between me and Freeman," she said emphatically. Maybe if she said it a few more times, it would totally sink in and take root in her heart. As it was now, the words just knocked around, unable to find purchase and then pushed out of the way when something sweet happened, like him stopping by to talk, wanting to go with her to look at her house. Then there were times when she wanted to turn away and forget she had ever met him. Like when he thought she should give up her house and her dreams of raising goats and making lotions and soaps and take on his dream instead.

"There can't be anything between me and Freeman," she said again. They had different dreams and different plans for their futures, and if something happened that ruined their precious friendship…now, that was something that she couldn't allow, not for anything in the world.

Chapter Eight

❧

"Nope," Jesse Raber said with a shake of his head. "Don't understand them one bit."

Freeman wasn't sure who brought up the subject, but it was something he was quite interested in. Women. And would men ever understand them? Surely a certain amount of understanding had to go into a marriage, but at the rate he was going he would have neither. Not understanding and certainly not a marriage.

Like tonight. He felt sure that he and Evie would ride to the singing together. When he had arrived at her house, he was told by Mattie that Evie, Naomi and Sarah Ann had already left together. Without him.

Jah, he had stewed on it all the way to the deacon's house where tonight's singing was to be held. Chris Peight was a good man, even if his wife, Imogene, was a little bit too talkative. They kept a tight rein on their son, Rudy, who at a tender seventeen wasn't allowed to do much more than he had before he turned sixteen. That was the thing about *rumspringa*. He had heard *Englischers* in town talking about Amish running wild, and he supposed some of them did. Truthfully an Amish child who had not yet joined the church could only get away with whatever their parents would let them get away with. For some, like Rudy, it wasn't much.

"You got it all wrong," Noah Peight, Rudy's cousin, chimed in. "You're not supposed to understand women. You're supposed to get along with them."

Jeremiah King lifted his cup of punch in salute. "Hear, hear."

A few agreeing cheers went up from the group of them.

"How am I supposed to get along with them if I don't understand them?" Abel Ebersol, Evie's cousin, asked.

That was exactly what Freeman wanted to know. He must not have been alone in that questioning, for the elation over Noah's comment quickly died to nothing.

"Take my advice on this," Zeke Byler started, "and you can quote me. Don't even try. Your life will be much easier."

A round of laughter rose. *Jah*, Freeman supposed it was all funny and a nice joke until you settled yourself on marrying someone and she refused.

"What happens if you ask someone to marry you and they turn you down?" he finally asked.

The group grew strangely quiet. Noise went on around them. The girls chattered on the other side of the room. A few people were still singing or practicing songs to one side, and another group of men were all carrying on about something else. Yet right there, in their little circle, it was as if all the noise had been sucked away.

Jeremiah cleared his throat. "I guess you're talking about Helen."

A few of the men grimaced as if they couldn't believe Jeremiah had the audacity to say her name in front of Freeman.

"No," Freeman said with a sad shake of his head. He started to say Evie's name, but somehow he couldn't throw it out like that. Strange how he didn't mind Helen's name tossed around, but his relationship with Evie…he definitely wanted to keep it more private. At least until it had some firm footing. He shook his head. "I guess I was talking hypothetically. Like what if you find a girl and you like her, but she doesn't like you back. Say someone like Naomi Ebersol. Or even her sister, Evie."

So much for being vague.

"I don't know about Naomi," Noah Peight said. "She's kind of scary."

A few of the guys nodded their heads, and honestly Freeman couldn't blame them. He'd accused Evie of being stubborn, but she was quietly stubborn. Naomi was in-your-face about it. She definitely had her own set of rules.

"And Evie," Noah continued. "I guess I never thought about Evie."

Freeman resisted the urge to grab him by the shoulders and shake him, demanding to know why. Then again, he didn't want any more attention on Evie than necessary. She was a hidden jewel. An Easter egg half buried in the grass. People were walking by, not even realizing it as they passed. But he had noticed. *Jah*, he had.

"I had a problem once and she helped me with it." Abel gave a quick nod. "Ripped one of Mamm's quilts, and I didn't want her to find out. She told me not to take it outside and I did. So, I knew she would be upset if she saw it. Evie fixed it, and I think it was better after she was finished than it was before I tore it up."

"She's handy all right," someone said.

She was handy. And beautiful. And smart. And overlooked. And always on the fringes. And worth more than everyone gave her credit for.

"What about your sister?" Jeremiah asked.

"Well," Abel continued. "If I'd had Faith do it, she would've held it over my head forever. Not Evie."

Freeman nodded, sure that if he had been in the same situation as Abel, his own sisters would've done the same. Yet he was amazed at all the problems Evie had solved for the people he was talking to, and all the lives that she touched on a weekly, daily, basis. Yet no one had thought about her as a life mate.

He knew why. Even though he didn't want to say it. He knew it was because of her crutches. She appeared fragile, not in a bad way, but in a fragile way. Amish women for the most part were strong, hardworking and able to stand on their own two feet, even if they were standing right behind the men they married. That was fine. That was how God intended. But just because she used crutches didn't mean she couldn't stand on her own two feet. Didn't mean she couldn't stand behind a man to support him.

He was keeping all that to himself. He

wouldn't want anyone else getting ideas about Evie. Not when he had yet to convince her to marry him.

"Just another thirty minutes." Naomi's voice was beseeching. Freeman was sure he'd never heard her sound so urgent. He inched closer, hating himself for eavesdropping yet somehow unable to stop it.

"I'm just so tired today," Evie said, closing her eyes as the word slipped from her lips. Freeman could see the lines of exhaustion on her face. It was a Sunday, a non-church Sunday, and no one did any unnecessary work on Sunday, but something had done her in.

"Twenty more minutes and we all ride home together," Naomi bargained.

"We're trying to get Mose King to ask Sarah Ann to ride home with him," Evie said. "Remember?"

"All the more reason to stay," Naomi said. "If we go now, Sarah Ann will come with us. If we stay, then she'll be here for Mose to ask."

"I don't want to mess that up," Evie said. "I finally got her to think about somebody else besides Judah Peachy."

"Kudos to you for that too," Naomi said.

Evie was shaking her head. "I guess I'll find a place to sit."

Naomi hid a triumphant smile in the guise of a worried nod. "Twenty minutes, tops." She started to turn away when Freeman sauntered up, casually as if he hadn't been listening to the last few minutes of their conversation. "I came to say bye."

Naomi spun back to look at him. "You're leaving?"

"*Jah*. I'm heading out." He hoped the timing of his leaving wasn't too obvious. Thankfully, Naomi seemed not to notice.

She turned back to her sister. "This is perfect! Evie, maybe Freeman can take you home." Back to him. "You will, right?"

He almost felt bad for her and the pleading in her voice. Almost. "Of course."

Evie was shaking her head. "It's okay. I can wait."

"That's dumb, sister. If you're tired and he's already heading in that direction…"

That was a stretch. He would have to drive past the turnoff to his house in order to take her home, then backtrack to get to his place. But as long as she went with him…that was all he cared about. He had missed her driving with him tonight. He wasn't sure why she had insisted on riding with her sisters, but this should do it. Taking her home tonight would definitely go a long way in showing everyone in the district that he was serious about Evie Ebersol. Eventually she would catch on as well. He wasn't going anywhere.

"He has to drive past his own driveway in order to take me home. That's not a good plan."

Naomi looked back to Freeman.

He shrugged.

"I'll make you an apple pie if you take her home."

"Naomi!"

"Raspberry rhubarb?" Freeman asked. He couldn't make this too easy on her.

"It's really not necessary," Evie protested. "I've already said I'll wait another twenty minutes."

But her sister was not listening. "Raspberry rhubarb it is."

"With that little crumbly stuff on top?"

"This is really not necessary," Evie said again. "Really. Not." She rubbed the line across her forehead right above her brows. A sure sign that she was fighting a headache. He knew it well. He also knew better than to call her out on it.

"Like a crisp?"

Freeman nodded. "*Jah*, but in a pie crust."

"Why is no one listening to me?"

Freeman didn't figure Evie expected anyone to answer her.

"Done," Naomi said.

"Ice cream?" He was really pushing it, but he figured he'd gone this far, and ice cream would make it a really good dessert.

Naomi eyed him shrewdly as if she knew he was up to something but then gave a quick nod, extending her hand for him to shake. "Deal."

"Get your jacket, Evie. Looks like I'm taking you home."

She supposed she could have refused, Evie thought as she sat in the buggy beside Freeman. How many times had they ridden home together like this? Too many to count. Never once had it felt different, like it did tonight. Important somehow. More important than she wanted it to be.

Jah, she should have refused, but she so desperately wanted to go home.

Her head had started to hurt about halfway through the singing. Not from the actual singing, but from all the efforts she was putting into avoiding Freeman. A lot of good it did her, she thought, as now she was not only with him, she was alone with him. And he had made sure that everyone at the singing knew that she was riding home with him.

"So have you given my proposal any thought?"

There it was: the real reason why she had avoided him and why she hadn't wanted to ride home with him. She had known deep down that he would do this. He would start to question her about that proposal. She had refused it. It had taken almost everything she had to tell him *no*. Yet she did it for his own good. She couldn't stand to be married to him only to have him resent her later on when she couldn't uphold her parts of the arrangement.

"I can't marry you, Freeman," she said. Somehow, she made her voice clear, succinct, the words strong. "I *won't* marry you, and I wish you would stop asking."

"You can't blame a guy for trying," he tossed back flippantly.

She pressed her lips together and stared straight ahead, but she could feel his gaze land on her. She only looked over at him when she felt it flick back to the road.

"I mean it though," he said, his voice suddenly turning serious. "I can't think of two better people to get married."

That would be true if they were only talking

about personalities and how well two people got along. And perhaps even the deep affection they had for each other. No way was she calling it love. Not the romantic type that people talked about in books, but a mutual respect and admiration, built on years of friendship and trust. Even that wasn't enough to make a marriage.

"So, what are you gonna do? Avoid me for the rest of your life?"

It was the last thing she wanted to do. "No," she said honestly. There was no way she could avoid him for the rest of her life. She could barely avoid him for anything. Somehow, she would have to ride this out until the novelty wore off or Helen came back. Whichever came first.

"You were avoiding me tonight," he said. "That's why you didn't want to ride with me to the singing or even home afterword, *jah*?"

She nodded miserably.

"I don't mean to make you uncomfortable," he said. His voice was soft and sincere. "I just want to spend time with you. You're my best friend. I can't spend time with you if you're avoiding me."

He made it sound so simple. "It's for your own good," she whispered in return.

"How so?" he asked. Up until that moment

Evie hadn't been sure he had heard her at all, her voice was so strangled and quiet it hardly pierced the night between them.

"It just is," she said, somehow sounding like a petulant three-year-old.

She couldn't tell him the truth. Her fears and dreams and every other part of her life that was wrapped up in Freeman Yoder. He thought he had a bang-up plan, but all it would do in the end was leave her heartbroken. She supposed there was a chance that everything would work out in her favor, but what if it didn't and Freeman was gone from her life? Or even worse, they were married forever, and he regretted his rash choice in a new bride. *Nee*. She couldn't have that at all.

She chanced a quick glance in his direction. He was shaking his head, at her she knew, but his eyes were trained on the road. "Over the years I've watched you fix things for everybody in this community. Some of the guys were even talking about it tonight."

Jah, that's her. The dependable Evie who was there to lend a hand in any way she could for everyone around her.

"Your cousin Abel was telling a story about ripping his mom's favorite quilt. You fixed it for him so that he didn't have to have Faith do it, because she would have held it over his head for eternity."

Evie remembered that quilt. Her aunt Janie would have skinned Abel alive, taking it out fishing and snagging it on a branch while toting it home. More than that, Evie remembered how much that blanket meant to Janie. "I didn't do it to keep Abel out of trouble," Evie explained. "I knew that Janie would be heartbroken. It was the last quilt her mother made before she died."

"That's what I'm talking about, right there," Freeman said. "That you even remember which was the last quilt that your dad's brother's wife's *mother* made before she died. Who does that?"

She shrugged. "Someone who cares, I guess. It's not like I'm special or anything."

"You sure are to Abel."

"That's not saying much," she said dryly. "Sometimes Abel can be an idiot."

Freeman chuckled. "And you tell it like it is," he continued.

She shook her head. "Not like Naomi."

"No," he said. "Not like Naomi. Which is a good thing. Honest, but not so brutal, and not so namby-pamby, agreeing with everything someone says either."

He was saying she had backbone, but she supposed that was ironic considering she had a spine defect. Yet she didn't feel like the mood was right to point it out to him.

"Did you happen to talk to Faith tonight?"

"Why are you changing the subject?"

Evie smoothed her hands over the quilt covering her legs. "Because I would rather talk about you and Faith than me."

"That's your problem, Evie, right there. You're always fixing things for everyone else. Yet you won't allow anyone to fix things for you."

"Who's going to do that?" she asked. "You?"

"I'm trying to." He said the words without accusation or blame, but she felt both land on her like sparks from a wildfire. "You keep blocking me every chance you get. Are you ever going to tell me why?"

Evie bit back a sigh. "No," she simply said, and willed the tears welling in her eyes not to fall.

Chapter Nine

"Hey, Evie."

She turned as her cousin Faith approached. "I thought I saw you come in."

Evie smiled. "*Jah.* I thought I might make myself a new dress." It had been a long time since she had made something for herself. Usually, she spent her time sewing for others. Not that she minded. She loved to sew, and she loved creating things for the people whom she loved.

"That's some lovely material," Faith said, her eyes on the deep aqua blue that Evie was fingering. "And…we got this in last Friday." She held up one finger and scurried behind the counter and into the back room, coming out with a bolt of dark berry red. Or maybe it was more of a pink. At any rate, it was simply gorgeous and a little bit bold for conservative Millers Creek. Yet somehow Evie was drawn to it.

Maybe because lately she had been feeling

more and more like the plain sister. Not that it
mattered. Not that it should matter. But Mattie, Sarah Ann and Naomi had such beautiful
blond hair, inherited from their mother. Anna
Grace Ebersol was reported to have had nearly
white hair when she was in school. Priscilla and
Lizzie both had dark hair like their father. Not
black like Faith's, but a beautiful dark brown
like chocolate, silky and fine. Then there was
Evie. The best she could say is that her hair
was brown. Just brown. Kind of like a wild
rabbit. Where her sisters either had gorgeous
blue eyes or gorgeous green eyes, Evie's were
hazel. Never making up their mind what color
they wanted to be and certainly not in the gorgeous category.

Looks aren't important, she reminded herself. But if she wore this color, she would definitely stand out. It was strange that she even
wanted to. It seemed like she had spent most of
her life trying to blend in. She always stood out
because usually when they went somewhere
she was the only person clanking around on
metal crutches.

"I'll take it."

"Five yards?" Faith asked.

Evie nodded and followed her cousin to
the cutting counter. "Did you have fun at the

singing last night?" Evie asked, finally getting around to the subject matter she came to talk to her cousin about. Freeman.

"Oh, *jah*." Faith's smile was bright and sunny. Her blue eyes flashed with joy. "It was a lot of fun."

"Did you happen to talk to anyone special?"

The bolt of fabric thunked against the counter as Faith unrolled it, stretching the fabric out against the yardstick to measure the correct amount. "No. No one special."

Honestly, sometimes it was like pulling teeth. Better be direct. "What about Freeman Yoder?"

Faith didn't miss a beat. "No," she said as she grabbed her scissors and started cutting the fabric.

"Not at all?" How disappointing, or at least that's what she was going to tell herself. There was a little jump in her heart, some sort of weird excitement and thrill that she got from her cousin not talking to Freeman. Which was utterly ridiculous.

"You know what," Faith said, her eyes wide. She took the small moment to pin the receipt to the folded fabric, before pushing it across the counter toward Evie. "Freeman will love this color on you."

Okay, this was not going at all as planned. "It might look even better on you," Evie said. "I'm sure Freeman would like that too."

Faith had been bustling around grabbing a sack and ringing up Evie's purchase, only stopping when she heard Freeman's name once more. "Why would you say that?"

Nothing like being put on the spot. "Well, I thought I saw you talking to Freeman the other day." It wasn't quite a fib, more an exaggeration of the truth.

Faith frowned. Evie couldn't help but notice that even with a look on her face that was not so positive, her cousin was still beautiful. Perfect. "Are you saying you think Freeman Yoder likes me?"

Again on the spot, Evie shrugged and tried to make her words come out in a breezy tone, nonchalant and unimportant. "Maybe."

"Oh, no, no, no, no, no." Her cousin shook her head. "Everybody knows Freeman Yoder likes you."

Evie felt heat rising into her cheeks until she was certain she was the color of the fabric she had just bought. "No, he doesn't. At least not as anything other than a friend."

"I've always wondered..." Faith said, crossing her arms and shifting her weight to one foot. "You know… I mean, he and Helen were such a thing for so long and who even knew what they had talked about to each other?"

Evie didn't have to ask her cousin what she meant. She knew. There were too many differences between Helen and Freeman for anyone to look at the relationship and immediately accept it. Still, it was nice to know she wasn't the only one in the valley who questioned such an arrangement.

It was something that Evie had thought about ever since that first singing when Freeman took Helen home and forever established them as a couple in the eyes of their community. Freeman was the salt of the earth, a hardworking man. Not that Helen was a bad person, but she and Freeman weren't alike. She was more concerned about what color anyone wore to church, especially if it wasn't blue. Then what shade of blue it was when they did wear blue. For some reason, there was a tradition in their community and most women wore blue to church.

Freeman wasn't like that, concerned with what was on the surface.

"Helen can be very charming." And that was the truth. Which was another reason why if she came back and wanted to marry Freeman, Evie figured he would fall right back into her arms.

"But you and Freeman," Faith continued, her expression growing a bit dreamy. "That I can see."

Evie hadn't thought it possible, but her face grew even hotter. She had to wonder if she would ever return to the same temperature and color she had been before. "That's ridiculous," she scoffed, but her voice broke on the last bit.

"Oh, no," Faith said with a shake of her head. "I've seen how he looks at you."

"At me?" She had never noticed Freeman looking at her. She had never seen any man looking at her. She was skimmed over, the fixer, never part of the equation.

"He took you home from the singing last night."

Evie didn't want to think about that. What was done was done. She couldn't stop the incorrect assumptions people were bound to make about them. Thankfully it wasn't a big singing like the ones that usually happened after a church service, but it was big enough. It wouldn't be long before everyone in the district would be talking about her and Freeman. Not to them or even in front of them, but where they couldn't hear. Behind raised hands and in whispered voices. There was nothing more intriguing than trying to figure out secret relationships. It was a puzzle their community couldn't help but try to unravel.

"Only because I needed a ride home. Naomi and Sarah Ann—" She broke off. "Never mind." She could already tell that her cousin didn't believe a word she was saying. That was the problem with keeping a relationship a secret. When a couple had been together as long as Freeman and Helen, the signs were always there. When the relationship was new, just starting out and the couple was trying to downplay what was happening between them, they said the exact same things that Evie was saying to Faith. It was a lost cause. Big singing or not, she was fairly certain that by nightfall everyone would be thinking that she was courting Freeman Yoder.

Evie was more than a little confused as she drove home from the fabric store. Right now, it seemed everything that she could do to prove that she and Freeman weren't dating made it look like they were dating all the more. There was no way he could find another person to date if everyone thought they were going out. Wasn't that what they called a catch twenty-two? Maybe. It was a catch something, that was for sure.

As soon as she got home and put the horse and buggy away, she carried her fabric into the house and started setting up on the kitchen table.

"What you doin'?"

Evie smiled down at tiny Bethann, her sister's oldest daughter. "I'm gonna make myself a new dress."

"Pwetty," Bethann replied.

Evie only nodded in return.

"I want to help!"

"Of course you can help," Evie said. She nodded toward the end of the table, the spot where Mattie usually sat. "Climb up in that chair, and I'll get you some scissors."

It took only a second to find the safety scissors that Mattie kept around for the girls. She returned to the dining area to find Bethann seated as instructed, swinging her legs and sucking her thumb as she waited.

"Okay, little girl," Evie said, laying out the pattern on top of the fabric. "Let me get this cut out, and I'll have a piece for you to work on, okay?"

Still sucking her thumb and swinging her legs, Bethann nodded. She waited patiently for Evie to finish her task.

"What are you doing?" Mattie asked, coming in the room from upstairs. She held baby Davida over one arm as she patted her tiny back with the other.

"I'm making a new dress," Evie said. "Beth-ann is helping."

Mattie continued to rock the baby back and forth and pat her back, obviously trying to re-lease a gas bubble. At least now, Davida wasn't crying. The poor child was sensitive. She didn't like baths. She didn't like putting on clothes. She didn't like her diaper changed. Hopefully, and with any luck quickly, she would outgrow some of that sensitivity.

"Pretty fabric," Mattie said, easing up to the table to rub the fabric between the thumb and forefinger of her free hand. Then she went back to patting Davida's back once more.

"I thought so," Evie replied.

"Once you get it cut out, set it to one side. It's time to milk the goats."

Already? It felt like they had just milked the goats. Though Evie was getting better each time she went out to help, she was nowhere near ready for a herd of her own. Definitely not a herd the size of Mattie's, but even when she did the math on how many goats were out there now, and how long it took her to milk them by herself, well, it didn't add.

"What's wrong?" Mattie asked. She shifted baby Davida to her shoulder, rubbing and bouncing as she waited for Evie's answer.

"Nothing," Evie murmured.

"If you don't want to milk the goats anymore, that's fine with me."

"It's not that," Evie said, neatly folding up the fabric with the pattern pinned to it so she could wait until she had time to sew the pieces together.

"Then what is it?"

Evie shook her head. "Nothing. Really." So maybe nothing was an understatement. Truly there was almost too much bothering her to lay it all on Mattie at one time. She had been looking forward to making the dress. Sitting down and concentrating on the fabric and the stitches put everything in its place. All the little pieces that were second nature to her somehow helped her center herself. It was almost like a prayer.

"Okay, girlie. We need to put this aside for a bit. You can come back when we're done with the goats. *Jah?*"

Obediently, Bethann placed the scissors to one side and started folding her fabric much in the same fashion that Evie had folded hers.

"Down now." Evie held out one hand as

Bethann stood in the seat of the chair, clasped her fingers in her own and jumped to the floor.

"Run upstairs and find Naomi." Evie turned and found Mattie staring at her, a strange look on her face. "What?"

"You'll make a great mother."

Evie shook her head. She would never be a mother, because she loved someone whom she could never marry. She would never know if he loved her like he loved Helen. She couldn't go through her life with that sort of uncertainty.

Fifteen minutes later, Evie dragged herself outside to help Mattie milk the goats. Two hours later she dragged herself back into the house, wondering if she would ever get the hang of this. *Jah*, she was faster than she used to be. Some of it had to do with the fact that the goats knew her now and weren't afraid of her crutches anymore. Now they seemed okay with her carrying out what they essentially considered Mattie and Naomi's chore.

She collapsed in the armchair and set her crutches on the floor to the side where no one would trip over them. Then she let out a long sigh. "So how much milk does each goat produce?"

Mattie came out of the kitchen, hand towel draped over her shoulder and washrag in her hands. She came over to where Evie sat and handed her the wet cloth. "Here," she said. "About two gallons or so. Depends. Why?"

"It's a lot of work," Evie said, choosing each word carefully. She didn't want her sister to think that she couldn't handle the responsibility. She prayed every day for strength and guidance. God would get her through. "I know there's no way I can milk as many goats as you do every day, but I don't think I'm going to need that many to make lotions and soaps."

Mattie waited until Evie had wiped her hands on the wet rag, then she handed her the dish towel to dry them. They used antiseptic and things in the barn, but it always felt good to come back in the house and wash her hands for real. Yet Evie was so tired today she didn't think she could make it all the way into the kitchen. She loved her sister all the more for not asking or fussing as she brought her the makeshift handwashing towel.

"So how much are you going to need for each item?" Mattie bustled back into the kitchen and came out sans the towels. She perched on the couch across from Evie. Charlie, who had followed Mattie into the kitchen both times and out of the kitchen both times, bleated her displeasure. Then she hopped up on the couch next to her mistress.

"That's the thing," Evie said. "I'm not exactly sure."

Of course, Naomi picked that time to come down the stairs, baby Davida cradled in her arms. "You want to make goat milk lotions and soaps, and you don't know how much goat's milk you're going to need?"

When she put it like that...

It had been an idea that she had allowed to grow into a dream. It sounded fun and exciting and something she could do without anyone's help. But as far as the practicality of the entire endeavor... Well, that still had to be ironed out.

Making lotions and soaps was going to be the easy part. Not nearly as physical as milking goats. In her mind she had to be able to handle her herd before she truly dreamed of opening her business. The rest would be easy as pie.

"You can always go to the library and look it up," Mattie coached. "Maybe even get some recipes that you can use to start. You have to have amounts to go on before you can even decide how big your herd needs to be."

Once again, her pragmatic sister was exactly right. It wouldn't hurt one bit to get a jump start on that part of her plan.

Naomi rolled her eyes and handed the baby over to her mother, then turned her attention back to Evie. "You better find out quick."

Evie nodded.

Mattie sat down in the rocker and started to feed Davida.

"Have you ever even made soap? Or lotion?"

"Well, no." That hadn't seemed important. What could there be to making soap? But she knew she had gotten caught up in her dreams of independence and let the details go to the wayside.

"I suppose it's time to figure out that part too," Mattie said, gently stroking her baby's downy head.

"*Jah*, what if you hate it?"

She wasn't going to hate it, but it would be a good idea to give everything a trial run before she set the entire plan into motion. "I'm not going to hate it," she said out loud, as much to convince Naomi as to believe it herself. "I'm going to love it."

Chapter Ten

Apparently, it wasn't so imperative to remain quiet in the library these days, Evie thought as once again the group of *Englisch* girls burst out laughing.

Evie had gotten up extra early to get her chores done and to help Mattie with the goats, before heading off to the library to look for a book on making goat milk soaps and lotions. Currently, she had a stack in front of her. She was going through them, checking recipes and such, making sure she had the best one before she checked it out and took it home. She would have had a much easier time concentrating if the girls would stop being so loud.

Her head dropped a little farther over the book as the girls began chatting loudly. It seemed that the library had had some sort of event for a local author who visited and talked about their latest book, and the girls had come to hear them speak. Now that the event was over, the girls had their books signed and they should be leaving. Yet they were hanging out in the library, discussing the blond-haired girl's dog.

Evie looked up at the tiny pooch with his head barely sticking out of the top of the girl's tote bag. It was a large carryall, and plenty big enough for the dog, given the size of his head. The thing couldn't weigh more than five pounds. Maybe even less. Evie wasn't sure why the woman felt it necessary to carry the dog around in a purse with her everywhere. What happened when the dog had to go to the bathroom? She wanted to know, but not enough to interrupt their conversation and ask.

"I get it," the dark-haired girl said with a clap of her hands. "It's just like hers." She rattled off a name, and for a split-second Evie thought perhaps it was one of the girl's friends, but after they continued talking, she figured out it had to be some celebrity. A celebrity who had a large bag and a little dog and took it everywhere with her. Now all the other *Englisch* girls wanted the same large bag and the same small dog to carry around with them.

"I just love that he's not going to get any bigger. He will always be my widdle baby." She gave an exaggerated pout to punctuate her words.

"He's so little you can take him everywhere," the other girl said, scratching the dog behind the ears. He licked her hand for her efforts.

"I love having him with me all day," the first girl said. "But first I had to register him as an emotional support animal. That way most places can't turn me away when I want to bring him in with me."

"Brilliant," the dark-haired girl exclaimed.

"I know, right?" The blonde laughed as she said the words and thankfully the group of them moved toward the exit of the library, allowing Evie to have peace and quiet in which to work.

But her concentration was broken. She couldn't imagine carrying a dog around everywhere with her. She could barely keep up with her purse.

With a sigh Evie loaded the five books she had picked up into her backpack and slung it across her shoulders, using it as a means to transport them to the checkout desk. She needed to get back home, and what was the difference between returning one book in two weeks and returning five? This way she could look at them at her leisure and wouldn't have people standing, laughing and talking about dogs to interrupt her as she did.

Though she liked the looks of the little dog.

Small enough for her to handle, and with a seemingly sweet disposition. He would have to be if people allowed the young woman to cart the pooch all over town. And apparently they did.

Maybe Evie should get one for herself. So if she couldn't keep up with her handbag, she could put the tiny dog in a backpack and always have him with her.

I wonder how much a dog like that costs.

Surely that was the kind of canine that people purchased. Pure-bred like some of the Belgian horses in their area. But purchasing a dog meant contacting a breeder and she had no idea if there was even one in the valley.

As quickly as the idea came to her she allowed it to slip away. She didn't have time for such matters at the present time. She had soap and lotion to make.

The sun was shining brightly as she stepped out of the library a few minutes later. She placed her backpack on the passenger side of the buggy, then pulled herself inside and started for home. The warmth of the sun was uplifting, and until her mood shifted, she hadn't realized how sour it had been. She hated that. She didn't want to be a Negative Natty. She had always prided herself on having a positive attitude, but here lately it seemed as if she was faced with more and more disappointments and setbacks than ever before. When she got home, she would pray over it, she decided. She could pray right now, she supposed as she drove, but she hated having to split her attention between making sure the horse stayed on the road and God.

Then when she got home there was another buggy in the driveway. She set the brake and climbed down. "Hi, Freeman."

He was on his feet in a heartbeat, jumping off the porch and rushing over to her. "I've been waiting for you."

Obviously. Then there came that sour mood once more. She pushed it back down and smiled at him sweetly. "I didn't know you were coming today."

He shook his head. "I didn't either. I came to apologize for Sunday night." He took her backpack from her hands, and she bit back the argument that she could do it herself. She could do it herself, but that didn't mean she had to prove it every time she had a bag to carry.

"What about Sunday night?" she asked. Together they made their way over to the porch. He sat next to the little table where Mattie served lemonade to visitors.

Evie eased down into her chair as she waited for Freeman to answer.

"I wanted to tell you that I'd been listening to you and Naomi talking before I came up and told you I was going home."

"So, you weren't going home when you told us that you were going home?"

"I was going by to get something to drink, and I heard your conversation. I figured that was a perfect chance to take you home."

And get the whole district talking about them.

Evie sighed. "It's going to be terrible when Helen comes back, and she thinks I've been encroaching on you."

He frowned. "Encroaching?"

She shook her head. "It doesn't matter. If she thinks the two of us have taken up, and she comes home and decides that she wants to marry you—"

"Evie, I have no intention of ever marrying Helen. Not ever." Freeman scooped her hand out of her lap into his own large, calloused palms. His touch was warm, thick and sweet like honey, and she felt the tingle of it from the tips of her fingers all the way to her heart. How could one touch affect her so?

It took all the strength she had to pull her fingers from his grasp. "No," she said. "No."

She picked up her bag, slung it across her

shoulders and started for the door. She couldn't do this. She just couldn't.

She heard him rise to his feet behind her.

"Don't you dare follow me inside, Freeman Yoder. I've had enough of this nonsense. Go home!"

Thankfully, he did as she asked and stayed on the porch, and she slammed the door behind herself with as much force as she could, all while keeping Charlie still inside.

She had things to do. She wasn't up for all his mushy-gushy whatever about getting married because he was trying to save face because Helen left. She was his best friend. Except she felt more and more, every day, like he was using her. She hated the feeling. They might be best friends. But she didn't have to participate in his foolishness. He could do that all by himself.

She dumped her backpack onto the table and pulled out the first book her fingers touched. She was going to make soap. Right now, this very minute. That way she would know how much soap she would have and how much she was going to need and whether or not she could make it work on her own. Judy wouldn't hold the house forever. And Evie wanted that piece of property with every fiber of her being.

As quickly as she could, she made her way to

the pantry and retrieved the box she had stored there. She had been collecting soap-making things for the last week. Who knew so many things were needed? Lye, water, fragrance, oils, not to mention goat's milk. She hoisted the box onto the dining room table and started flipping through the book. The instructions were simple. Find a big pan, use a ventilated room, mix everything together. Though there was no mention of when to add the goat's milk. And she couldn't say the room was well ventilated. So, she opened the window on the other side of the table, letting in the fresh air. That should do it.

She started mixing things up. Then all of a sudden, this terrible smell wafted up from the pan. *Ew.*

Was it supposed to smell like that? The soap kept rising in the pan and she kept stirring, all the while trying to flip through the book to see what exactly she was supposed to do when it started to stink. It was difficult, stirring and flipping at the same time. Plus, she really didn't think she had the right book. This one didn't appear to be about making goat milk soaps. It was about making regular soap. How hard could it be to switch from one to the other? Maybe she should've done this when she wasn't mad at Freeman.

"What in the world is that smell?" Mattie came in holding her nose.

"I don't know," Evie wailed. "I can't find anything in the book, and I can't stop stirring it because it keeps getting—ow!" She touched her arm to the side of the metal pan she was using to mix her soap. It burned! Like a hot stove. She was certain she would have a mark there this afternoon.

"Are you okay?" Mattie came closer, still fanning her hand in front of her nose.

"Don't touch this pan," Evie warned, still furiously stirring. The book had made it look so simple, but it seemed that there was more to soap making than a bunch of recipes.

"Oh, gross." Freeman came into the house, swinging the door wide and back again to get some of the smell out of the living room. "That stinks."

Charlie seemed to be biding her time and waiting for the right moment to sprint outside, but Mattie quickly opened another window and scooped the goat into her arms.

"I don't think it's supposed to smell like that," Freeman said. His words were hollow sounding, since he had pinched his nose closed with the fingers of one hand.

No, it wasn't supposed to smell like that.

She didn't need to read it in any book to know that something was horribly wrong. The soap was supposed to smell good, like the lavender oil that she added, but whatever went wrong and caused the awful smell was more powerful than her essential oils. It was a mess. A failure. A catastrophe.

She continued to stare at the pot of useless soap ingredients as if trying to will them to a success.

"I mean, it reeks." Freeman chuckled as he said the last word.

"I thought I told you to go home," Evie snapped.

"Evie." Mattie turned, her voice admonishing.

But Evie had had enough. Finally, the concoction in the large stock pot she had used to mix all the ingredients stopped rising. Evie tossed the spoon on the table with the rest of the mess. She had read the instructions—twice—and still the soap was a failure.

"You should apologize," Mattie told her. As the oldest, she was always telling them what to do.

The last thing Evie wanted to do was apologize. Even though she was acting rudely. Freeman was doing her in. How was she supposed to resist him if he was constantly underfoot? It wasn't fair.

"I'm sorry," she said, somehow managing to keep the tears from her voice.

Then she grabbed her crutches where they were braced in the corner. With as much aplomb as she could manage, she made her way to the downstairs bedroom she had claimed as her own, leaving Mattie and Freeman to stare after her in disbelief.

Freeman was only vaguely aware that his expression matched Mattie's as he watched Evie disappear down the hallway. He had never known her to act this way. The door slammed behind her, and he turned to Mattie. "What's wrong with her?" He meant it sincerely, and yet somehow it came out accusatory. "I mean she's not like this. I don't understand what I've done wrong."

Before Mattie could answer, the door opened, and Naomi scuttled in and quickly closed it behind her so Charlie couldn't escape. She wrinkled up her nose and squinted her eyes as the terrible odor hit her. "What is that smell?"

"I can't tell you exactly," Mattie said. "Evie tried her hand at making goat milk soap and… I'm not sure. I'm supposing everything needs to be tossed out." She gave a slightly horrified look at the table where Evie's mess still sat. "Make sure the girls don't get in it. I'm thinking maybe you should give it a break for a little while."

"I can't." He shook his head as if trying to rattle things back around right. It didn't work. "I bought the Hostetler farm and got everything set up and ready. All I need is a wife, and I thought Evie was going to be that wife."

Out of the corner of his eye he saw Naomi and Mattie share a look.

"Fine. There was a time when I thought that person would be Helen, but ever since I've put down a deposit on that property it's been Evie. Always Evie."

"This doesn't have anything to do with the promise, does it?"

Freeman whirled around to look at Mattie. "She told you?"

"Samuel did."

Freeman's hope deflated as quickly as it came. "I don't understand. I just don't get why she doesn't want to marry me."

He shifted uncomfortably as he watched the sisters once again share some kind of coded look. He had no idea what it meant.

"What?"

"You shouldn't mention the promise so much to her," Mattie started diplomatically.

"Why not?" The promise was the whole basis for this, the promise was what started it all. That promise was what made him see the truth for what it was, the path he needed to take and all that.

"No woman wants to believe a man only wants to marry her because he made a promise when he was six years old."

"I—" Freeman started, not sure of how to respond, but feeling the need to all the same.

"It's sweet and all," Naomi jumped in. "Really sweet, I guess. But you didn't love her then, and you made a promise. If you want her to know you love her now, you have to make a different promise."

"A different promise?" *A different promise?* A promise was a promise was a promise. Why did it have to be different now? He closed his eyes and shook his head, trying to bring about some clarity in this matter, but none was coming. "I guess," he said.

Naomi shook her head at him. "No 'I guess.' If you want her to fall in love with you now and you want her to know that you're sincere now, you have to make a different promise than the one you made then."

A different promise. Was it as simple as that? He had no idea, but one thing was certain. He couldn't leave without talking to Evie first.

Jah, she was mad as a wet hen, but he couldn't go home until she knew that he forgave her for snapping at him and...

Well, the *and* was the part where things got muddled.

"I'm going to talk to her," he said, ignoring the concerned looks that passed between Mattie and Naomi.

He rapped twice on the door before easing it open. "Evie?"

"Come in," she said, her tone anything but inviting. But as far as he was concerned it was a start.

He stepped inside her room, his gaze immediately falling on her.

He wasn't sure what he was expecting, but he had truly never seen his spunky Evie like this.

She had apparently thrown herself across the bed, for she pushed into a sitting position when he entered.

"I'm sorry," she said again. She used the back of one hand to wipe the moisture from her cheeks.

He pulled the straight-backed chair she had sitting by the door toward her and sat in it. She didn't pull away when he took her hands into his. That was a good sign. He was certain of it.

"I'm the one who's sorry, Evie. I shouldn't have laughed. But I truly wasn't laughing at you. More at the situation."

"I don't find the situation all that funny either," she admitted.

This might be harder than he realized. He took a deep breath and started again. "Did I ever tell you about the first time I drove Dat's buggy to town all by myself?"

She shook her head.

"Something spooked the horse, and I ran into the railing there at the hardware store. You know, the one that surrounds the parking lot? Put a half-inch deep scratch all down the side of the carriage. Dat was so mad." In fact, he didn't think he'd ever seen his father that angry since.

"What happened?"

"A lot of things," Freeman said. "We repaired the buggy. I had to repaint the railing, and Dat didn't let me drive alone for two months afterward."

"You never said anything."

He grinned though the action felt sheepish. "I didn't want anyone to know because I was embarrassed. But you want to know the best part?"

She nodded, patiently waiting for him to finish his tale.

"I didn't stop driving. I just kept practicing until I got it right."

"I'm not sure this is the same thing," she protested.

"It's exactly the same thing."

She waited three full heartbeats before responding. "I want this so badly."

"Then you shall have it," he solemnly promised. A new promise just for her. "Because you're smart and brave and you'll figure it out."

A small smile broke through and he caught a glimpse of the girl he knew among all the despair in front of him. "You think so?"

He smiled in return. "I know it for a fact."

Chapter Eleven

Evie sighed as she pulled the buggy to a stop in front of Mattie's house. She waited a moment longer, resting while she could.

She had gotten up that morning early to read through the book on soap making, only to discover she had checked out the wrong ones. She had been so distracted by the *Englisch* girl with the little dog in the big purse that she had picked up the wrong stack of books.

Of course, there wasn't a good way to make goat milk soap with a regular soap-making book. Having five of them on the same subject was surely no help either. So, she had gone into town to get the correct books. She needed to try her experiment once more. She had to know the process of making soap to see how much she should charge, what she needed, how long it would take, and everything else that went along with it. She couldn't jump into this feetfirst, it was going to take a little practice. Just like Freeman had told her.

Freeman. Yesterday had almost ended in disaster. But they had apologized to one another then he had left. But not before offering to help her clean up the mess her first attempt at soap-making had caused. She had shooed him away and her sisters too. It was her mess, and she would clean it up. And any that followed.

But now…she knew the moment she set foot inside the house, her sister would be telling her that it was time to go milk the goats again. It wasn't that she was afraid of hard work. She simply got tired quicker than most. That was one of the worrisome things about having her broken body.

"It's the body God gave you," she said, quoting her mother as she eased herself down to the ground. "Be thankful for it."

And she was. "Thank you, God for my beautiful life. Amen."

Evie retrieved her pack full of books from the back of the buggy and made her way inside the house.

Charlie bleated out a welcome as she stepped inside and shut the door behind her.

"There you are," Naomi said from the couch.

"Shhh," Mattie said in an urgent whisper.

"Keep it down. If you wake up the girls, you're taking care of them. All three of them. All by yourself."

"Where have you been?" Naomi asked, though her voice was much quieter this time.

"I went to the library to exchange the books so I can try making my soaps again. The ones that I had checked out didn't have recipes for goat milk soaps."

Mattie nodded at Naomi. "See? I told you."

Evie sat her bag down and turned to face her sisters. "Everything else all right?" she asked.

Mattie nodded. "Just in time to milk the goats."

Evie bit back a sigh. Of course it was.

It was Thursday night, and of course the buddy bunch was getting together to celebrate... Thursday night. After everything her sisters had talked to her about that morning, Evie knew she couldn't skip out. Plus, she had to help Sarah Ann capture Mose King's attention. Once again she felt like she was failing on both accounts.

Maybe tonight she could figure out a way to get Mose to take Sarah Ann home. It wouldn't be quite as momentous as him taking her home from a singing, but it would still be a step in the right direction. But how?

Evie walked with her sisters around the side of Aaron Byler's house. Truthfully, it was Amanda Byler's house since Aaron had died. Amanda was Samuel's mother and had agreed to host the Thursday night buddy bunch get-together for one of her other sons, Zeke. Zeke was twenty, in the middle of his *rumspringa* and showing no signs of settling down anytime soon. Evie couldn't help but wonder what Amanda thought of it all. Samuel had left for an extended period of time and Daniel had died. AJ, the oldest Byler son, had never married though no one around knew why, and now Zeke looked as if he was going to take his slow sweet time joining the church. They couldn't get married unless they joined the church. Who knew how long that would take?

Before his death, Aaron Byler had built a bonus room at the back of the house, a place for them to hold church and not be quite so crowded. It also kept people from tramping in and out of the house all day on that special Sunday. Some folks had fussed about it because they considered that like a church building, but Amanda had set up a canning business inside the space thereby turning it from church to church and work. Oh, there were still a few grumbles, but for the most part everyone let it drop. It was the thing these days, whereas they used to all have church in their homes or their barns, whichever had the most room. Now folks seem to be building on annexes, separate spaces. Adding to their barns. So they would have more room to accommodate the congregation. There were those who said it was just a hop, skip and a jump from setting up a chapel somewhere, but she supposed as long as there were some holdouts who didn't build on and insisted on having church in their homes, the chapel idea would fall flat.

"I don't know what to do," Sarah Ann said, nervously running her hands down the front of her apron and dress.

"Be yourself," Lizzie said. She and Sarah Ann had swung by Mattie's house to pick up Evie for the night. Naomi was staying home to help Mattie with the girls, and then she wanted to repaint the bedroom the three of them would share.

"Am I supposed to do that?" Sarah Ann said. "How can I be anyone else?" She stopped dead in her tracks. "Maybe this is a bad idea. Maybe I should just go home."

Evie stopped next to Sarah Ann and braced her elbow on one of her crutches as she reached for her sister's hand. She clasped her fingers into her own and squeezed them softly. "Breathe," she said. "You're putting way too much emphasis on this. Everything is going to turn out the way that everything is supposed to turn out."

Sarah Ann sucked in a deep breath and let it out slowly, her shoulders sagging with effort. "Right. What will be, will be. Isn't that what the *Englisch* say?"

"Let's stick with God's will for tonight." Evie chuckled. "And don't go worrying about Mose King or Judah Peachy or any of them. Go in and have fun."

"Don't worry. Have fun."

Evie smiled at her sister. "You got it."

Once again, they started for the bonus room in back of the Byler house.

"What about you and Freeman?" Lizzie asked.

Evie swung her gaze from Sarah Ann to Lizzie. Both nodded encouragingly.

"How do you know about—"

"Naomi told us," Sarah Ann said.

Evie shook her head. "Can there not be any private matters in this family?"

Lizzie chuckled. "Apparently not."

"Well, there's nothing for me to do with Freeman. Regardless of all the chatter the other night."

"Shouldn't you let him decide?" Sarah Ann asked.

Evie stopped. "You're absolutely right," she said to Sarah Ann. "That's on the off chance that he really cares about me. He only wants to marry me because he made that stupid promise to me twenty years ago. How could I hold him to that?"

"I don't think you're holding him to anything, if that's what he's insisting he wants to do." Lizzie gave a negligent shrug as if her words explained everything.

To a certain point, Evie supposed they did. But to have that hope... She couldn't allow herself. It left too much room for heartbreak when and if Helen came back.

Though she had been gone for weeks, as far as Evie knew no one had heard from Helen at all. She was definitely living it up in Lancaster, but Evie knew, somehow, deep down, that Helen would be back. When that happened, the last thing Evie wanted was for her good friend to find her running around with her ex-fiancé. It wasn't right.

The party was just gearing up as they walked into the room. It was a large empty space with a couple of tables along one side and a stove at the end. Before his death, Evie had heard

David, her sister's late husband, talk about the plans his father had for the room. How there was going to be a bathroom added and maybe even an extra bedroom in case someone wanted to spend the night, but he had never gotten around to making that a reality. In fact, it was David who set up the stove and canning area for his *mamm*.

She glanced around the room briefly, noting that Freeman wasn't there yet. She was anxious to see him again. To tell him that she had gotten the correct books for making goat milk soap. That she had taken the next steps to realizing her dream, just as they had talked about.

"Don't be so anxious," Lizzie whispered under her breath. At first Evie thought she was talking to her, but then she realized Lizzie was talking to Sarah Ann.

"I'm only nervous because you keep telling me I'm not ever going to get married."

"I only say that because I am your sister, and I'm supposed to."

They had been talking side by side, out of the corner of their mouths, not facing each other. But that did it. Sarah Ann whirled around to look at Lizzie in complete disbelief. "That's the worst thing I've ever heard."

Lizzie shrugged and smiled. "If I can't tease you who can?"

Sarah Ann seemed to think about it for a moment, then turned to Evie.

Evie shot her a small smile. "Don't look at me. Mattie did the same thing to me for years. Claimed it was for my own good."

"See?" Lizzie said. "It's my sisterly duty. Besides, I only tell you that because I love you."

"Well then," Sarah Ann started smartly, "there are times when I wish you didn't love me quite so much."

The girls all laughed as they made their way to the punch table to get something to drink. Food had already been laid out, chips and dip and vegetables. Somebody had made some kind of pinwheels with cream cheese and tortillas. Lizzie was the only one who managed to grab a plate and get a bite. Evie was too nervous, and she supposed Sarah Ann was as well. Well, it didn't help that Mose was already there. Evie was certain that Sarah Ann didn't want to be seen chomping down on messy foods when there was a chance of him looking up from across the room and catching her in a compromising position.

"Evie." Rebecca Yoder sidled up and threaded

her arm through one of Evie's. "I love that dress."

It was the berry-colored fabric that Evie had bought from Faith a few days before. She had finally managed to finish the garment between experiments of trying to make soap. In perfect time to wear it tonight.

Even if she made it herself, she had to admit that it turned out well. Probably one of her best dresses. Everything seemed to come together perfectly in the color that made her wishy-washy eyes look a smoky green, like mist over a meadow. Strangely enough it made her hair look a little darker, brought out red highlights she didn't know she had. All in all, she was pleased with the overall effect, and she wished she had three more dresses in the same color. It made her feel pretty for the first time in her life.

"Danki," she said, smiling at Rebecca. She wanted to ask Freeman's sister where he might be tonight, but she didn't want to seem too anxious to see him. Even if she desperately needed to apologize.

"Where's Freeman?"

She could have slapped her hand over her own mouth to keep this question from escaping, but there it was, out in the open. Yet Rebecca didn't seem surprised at all. "He's going to stay home tonight. He was packing up stuff to move to the farm. I can't believe he actually bought his own farm."

"Me either," Evie said, even though she knew it had been his dream for years. A dream he was finally getting to realize.

"So, he's not coming tonight at all?"

Rebecca shrugged. "I don't know. I don't think so," she said with a scrunch of her nose. "He wasn't dressed to come out when we left." She gave another small shrug. "You know Freeman."

That she did. Or she thought she did. She had expected him to be here tonight. He was always at the buddy bunch parties. He and Helen had never missed one for as long as she could remember, and he had kept it up even after Helen left. All the way until tonight.

"I heard from Esther that Helen is having a great time in Lancaster."

"She is?" Evie tried not to feel disappointed that her best friend had called her sister and not her, but it made sense. Still, she would've loved the opportunity to talk to Helen. Then again, with the way her mouth seemed to be running off tonight, it might be a good idea if she stayed away from such a conversation. She might be asking Helen all sorts of things about Freeman, their relationship and her intentions.

"You didn't hear this from me, but Esther said she thought Helen might have met someone there."

Met someone? Of course she met some—

"Like a man?"

Rebecca tilted her head back and forth as if to say, *Who knows?*

"Does Freeman know?"

"I didn't have the heart to tell him," Rebecca said. "If you ask me, he's much better off without her."

As far as Evie knew, Rebecca and Helen had never been close. This proved it.

"You two are much better suited for one another."

Evie felt that rise of heat in her face once more. "I don't know…" She trailed off, unable to finish any thought she had. Had Freeman said something to Rebecca about the promise he had made to her? Or was she assuming that since they were such good friends there was a possibility of more to the relationship? Or maybe she thought it could grow into something more. Then there was the fact that he had taken her home from the singing last week.

"It's okay," Rebecca said with a twinkling smile. "Your secret's safe with me."

Secret? What secret was Rebecca talking about? Evie desperately wanted to know, but not enough to actually ask her. That would open up a huge can of worms that Evie wasn't sure she was prepared to dig through.

Can of worms. Ew. Yet, that's exactly what it was: wriggling, wiggling, slimy ideas and promises and all sorts of other untrustworthy things that couldn't be sorted out easily. And all of it covered in dirt.

She shook her head at her rambling thoughts. She wouldn't go up and talk to Rebecca, so Evie had been stewing on the words for nearly an hour. The party was in full swing now and Freeman had yet to show up. Evie tried not to appear overly disappointed by the fact. As the night wore on, she could tell he was not coming. The minutes ticked off, each one bringing the party closer to its end. She knew he wouldn't bother at that point. It was too late, and she needed to be okay with that.

She had found a chair and sat down at the end of the refreshment table, within arm's reach of the chips and dip and celery. Three chips to one celery stick was her ratio of discipline. She could sit and eat chips and dip all night, but she wouldn't let herself.

Esther came up, dragging Lizzie by the hand. "Come on. I want you on my team."

"Team?" Lizzie asked, stumbling behind her. She cast one looked back at Evie then turned to face forward once more.

"For playing volleyball," Esther said.

Just when Evie was starting to feel a bit normal. Now she wanted to go home. It was one thing to go to a volleyball game and not be able to participate, but another to be at a party and have games break out that left her even further on the sidelines.

How she wished Freeman was here.

Chapter Twelve

He set the box on the kitchen counter and looked around the farmhouse that now belonged to him. His house. His farm.

It was supposed to have been the farm he shared with Helen. Now he wanted it to be the farm he shared with Evie, but he couldn't seem to convince her to give him—them—a chance. She had dreams of independence, and now his only hope was that she would move into the house, set up her business and feel successful. Once she knew she could do it, then he would ask her about marriage again. If he understood anything about Evie—and he knew his knowledge was questionable at best these days—he did understand her need to prove herself. He wanted the same. Which was the exact reason he had bought the Hostetler farm even though he didn't have a helpmate to share it with. He wanted the farm. He had to trust God that the rest would fall into place as His plan was revealed.

He opened the lid to the box and looked down at the plain white plates his *mamm* had picked out for him. He never realized how much stuff it took to run a household, things he never thought about, like spatulas and sheets, end tables and salt and pepper shakers. He had all that his *dat*'s home had and more. What did he think? That it was all going to be there and waiting for him when he moved in?

No. He had expected those things to come from a wife with a hope chest and a wedding with gifts to give the bride and groom a leg up in their lives together.

Instead, his mother had taken him on a shopping trip to Lewisville to get all the kitchen utensils and other things that he would need. Towels, throw rugs, a holder for his toothbrush.

He should have felt proud of all the work they had accomplished in the last couple of days. What had been an empty farmhouse with laminate flooring and dark green shades on the windows had turned into the start of a home. His home. His couch, his coffee table, his dinette table and his washing machine out on the porch. One other thing that he hadn't thought about when he decided to move out all on his own. Having to do his own laundry.

The house was set up for living and yet it still felt empty. He was fairly certain it had nothing to do with the blank walls with only a calendar from the co-op hanging right outside the kitchen. His mother didn't have much on the walls. A wedding sampler someone made her when she married his *dat* and a dreamy looking picture of praying hands to remind her daily to stop and pray often.

He needed a wife. And he wanted Evie. He could see her attempting to make soap at the little dinette set his aunt had given him to start off in his house. There was no window there like at Mattie's, so perhaps he would have to set her up a space on the back porch or at one end of the living room where they did have a window. Er, he had a window. As much as he wanted to, he couldn't count this space as belonging to her as well as him. Even though he had asked so many times.

With a sigh he shut the box, deciding to put the dishes up tomorrow. He had plenty of time for that. His mother had left him a stack of paper plates to use until he got settled, and he was going to take advantage of the convenience. No sense doing the dishes until he had to.

Freeman strolled over to the glass door that led out onto the covered back porch. All things considered, his was a fancy house. Small with only three bedrooms and barely enough room in the downstairs to hold church, but it had a few amenities that made it very special to him. One was this glass door leading outside. He could sit on his couch and see most of the backyard, including the space for the house garden.

He let himself out onto the porch. The sun was only now starting to set and the stars beginning to twinkle in the purple and pink sky. Off to each side of the lot were the fields where he would raise organic vegetables once he transferred the certification into his name. It would be a proud moment and one that he had been looking forward to for a while. Yet he wondered how much of the shine would be lost not having a wife at his side.

For so long he had believed that it would be Helen at his side, but that wasn't going to happen. And now he knew the truth.

It was Evie. It was always Evie. Evie was the woman he believed God had set aside for him. Why else, with all her love and bravery and grit and spunk, had no one snatched her up yet as their wife? Because God was patiently waiting for him to come to his senses and see what was hiding there in plain sight.

"Did you see?" Sarah Ann gushed as she flew in the front door at Mattie's house Friday morning. "Did you see?"

Evie looked up from unloading her box of soap-making supplies. She was going to do it today. Come what may, she was determined.

She set her measuring cups down next to the large stainless steel pan she was using to mix everything together. It wasn't quite as large as the previous pan she had been using, but currently that one was sitting on the stove full of chicken soup for tonight's supper. A small sacrifice to make as far as Evie was concerned. Mattie's chicken soup was so good.

"Did I see what?" Evie asked. Somehow, she felt as if she had missed something.

Sarah Ann sidestepped Charlie, who bleated in disappointment that Sarah Ann didn't bend down and scratch her behind the ears, and came toward Evie, her shoulders slumped in disbelief and disappointment. "Mose. Last night. You didn't see." Her tone bordered on heartbroken, and Evie immediately felt remorse. She *had*

missed something, but last night had been...
a disaster.

She'd been near tears when she left the get-together. She had expected to see Freeman, to be able to talk to him, but he wasn't there. Then everyone started playing volleyball and she had felt more left out than ever.

"Of course I did," Evie said. That was what they called a white lie, right? Not meant to hurt anyone. She couldn't stand that sad, dejected look on her sister's face after all they had been through in the situation with Mose.

But Sarah Ann was shrewd. She cocked her head to one side, her mouth twisted in a skeptical pout. "Oh, *jah*? What did he do?"

No way out of this one. Evie was caught. She had tried to save face, tried to spare her sweet sister's feelings, and it had backfired. Evie had lied to Sarah Ann and now she was going to have to tell the truth to get out of it. The truth, she knew, would make her sister even sadder. "Okay. I'm sorry. I didn't see."

Sarah Ann's mouth fell open in disbelief. "You were going to lie to me about it?"

"Sarah Ann, I'm sorry," Evie said. "I messed up. I should've never done that. I did not have a very good evening, and I apologize that I missed what was apparently a very good evening for you."

Sarah Ann mulled it over for a moment, then gave a quick nod. "I forgive you." Then she wrapped Evie in a tight, sweet hug.

When she pulled away, her eyes were dancing once more. "Well, first he asked me to be on his volleyball team, and then he high-fived me when we made a good play together. Then he got me a punch to drink after we were done playing." She sucked in a deep breath but said no more.

"That's it?" Evie immediately closed her eyes and shook her head at herself as Sarah Ann's expression fell. "No, that's not what I mean. I meant did anything else happen?"

Sarah Ann shifted in place, a loose-limbed, full-body shrug. "It's probably too early for him to ask me to drive home. Though it seems like he might be a little interested. Who knows? I might even get married before Lizzie."

Evie gave her a wan smile. "Wouldn't that be something?"

Once Sarah Ann got all her news out, her attention centered on Evie. "What's wrong, sister?"

Evie shook her head. How to even say what was troubling her? If she told Sarah Ann that

Freeman had asked her to marry him, Sarah
Ann would be like Naomi and Mattie, wondering what was wrong with her that she didn't
jump up and down and accept immediately.
Well, forget that jumping up and down part.
She supposed nobody expected her to do *that*,
but they would expect her, and did expect her,
to be more excited, grateful even and happy
that she could spend her life with someone as
fantastic as Freeman Yoder. Then again, Sarah
Ann might already know. The sisters didn't
usually keep secrets from one another. "Just a
bad spell," she said. "Plus, I've been trying to
learn how to make goat milk soap, and so far,
I'm not having much luck."

Sarah Ann waved a hand across the table
where Evie had stacked up all the ingredients
and utensils that she was going to need. Including the chunks of frozen goat's milk. She had
finally found out what the smell was the last
time she tried to make the goat milk soap. It
was due to the fact that the goat's milk over-
heated when the chemical reaction happened
between all the ingredients. One of the books
she got from the library suggested freezing the
goat's milk in ice cube trays before adding it
to the mixture to keep the product from over-

heating and scorching in the pan. "This is a lot of stuff," Sarah Ann said.

"I suppose it takes a lot of stuff."

"Are you going to make it now?" Sarah Ann asked, her excitement and awe nearly tangible.

Evie wasn't nearly so thrilled or confident that what she was about to do was even worth watching.

Nope. She was not going to let those negative thoughts enter her mind. She had God on her side. And her dreams. And He knew how important they were to her.

Yea, the Lord shall give that which is good.

"Can I watch?"

"Of course," Evie said, though the thought of having an audience did make her a tad nervous.

She opened the book to the proper page and started looking at it. More like squinting at it. She really ought to wear her glasses more, though she would never admit that out loud in front of any of her sisters. Or her dad. Or Freeman. The thing was she hated her glasses. She wasn't sure exactly why. Maybe because she already had enough tools and hardware to help her to get along. Having to use crutches or a walker to get around…she didn't need another appliance weighing her down. Which even in her own thoughts sounded a little silly. Still, she managed.

She narrowed her eyes a bit more in order to make out the amounts listed in the instructions. She was pretty sure the recipe called for a half a cup of lye mixture. *Jah*, that was a two. Definitely. She added the lye into the pan first like the book instructed so that it wouldn't splatter on her when she poured in the other ingredients. The water went in next with all the rest of the materials. Then all she had to do was stir.

"Phew." Sarah Ann waved a hand in front of her face. "That's strong."

Oh, no! Evie had forgotten to open the window. She gave the mixture one quick stir before leaving the wooden spoon next to the pan and quickly opened the window beside the table.

There. That should take care of it. The need for proper ventilation had completely slipped her mind. She would need to be more careful in the future.

"Does it always smell?" Sarah Ann asked.

"Some odor is normal. A least it doesn't smell like last time." Evie started stirring the soap mixture once more, but having to stop and open the window had put her a little bit behind. It was rising quicker than her stirring was pushing it back down. So, she stirred a little harder.

She could feel the heat of the pan. Perhaps it was too hot. Maybe if she added a bit more of the goat's milk it would cool it down enough to stop the soap mixture from rising plum out of the pan.

She put the spoon to one side, not careful in where she placed it. The thing landed right on top of the library book. She pushed it to one side but didn't think she had time to clean it up. It was probably ruined regardless of any efforts she could put forth now. So instead, she moved toward the goat's milk she had left.

Before she could get it into the pan, a big bubble of soap rose out of the top of the pan and burst, splattering everything. Thankfully, she had ducked her head, and the hot mixture landed on her prayer *kapp* instead of her face. Evie could feel the heat of it on her head through the thin layer of fabric. The soap was sprinkled on her arms and the lower part of her dress and apron. The bodice had taken the brunt and was shiny with the clear-ish soap she had tried to make.

Evie bit back the overwhelming emotions that threatened to spill out all over like the soap. Anger, frustration, depression, disbelief. Why couldn't she get this right? Why?

"Ow! What happened?" Sarah Ann looked at her arms, which were flecked with little bits of soap. Thankfully, she was far enough away that not much landed on her. Evie supposed that was a small blessing. She would hate for her sister to be badly burned because of her stupid mistakes.

Was that what happened? Had she made a mistake? Maybe added too much lye?

"I'm not quite sure," Evie said. She knew one thing: her prayer *kapp* was ruined. The material could barely stand up to the rain, much less hot soap. Though her dress and apron would probably survive, it would take multiple washings to get all the soap out.

"It was like a volcano." Sarah Ann's tone was filled with amazement and admiration. Evie deserved neither.

Unfortunately, volcano wasn't much of an exaggeration. Little flicks of soap to splotches big enough to be called outright blobs peppered everything within five feet or more.

"I guess the good news is that it's pretty easy to clean up soap, right?" Sarah Ann asked with a chuckle in her voice. "Because you don't even need to use soap."

Sarah Ann flashed her a bright smile. Yet Evie could feel herself crumbling. All she wanted to do was raise goats and make soap, but she had been failing miserably in all phases. She wasn't sure about her choices any longer. Her choices but not her dreams. She wanted that little house and that little lot and that little bit of property that she could call her own and be independent and happy. She wanted it so much she could almost taste it. It was right in front of her grasp, and she so desperately wanted it to be hers.

Tears welled and spilled over her lashes.

"Sister?" Sarah Ann moved toward Evie, carefully stepping around the splatters of soap that lay at their feet. "Oh, sister, what's the matter? Why are you crying?"

"Why can't I do this?" she asked. She really didn't expect an answer and Sarah Ann was unable to give one. Instead, her sister wrapped her in a hug and patted her on the back. "There, there," she cooed, but the words didn't soothe Evie. Not in the least.

What was she doing wrong? Why couldn't she get this right? She needed to get this right. She had to. If she was going to survive on her own, she had to have a job, something she could do. Soap making seemed like the perfect plan, and yet she couldn't manage to follow the recipe and make even one bar of soap without some disaster or another.

And milking the goats. That was coming a bit easier with practice but not easy enough for her to be able to take care of her own herd.

Why was she continually making a mess of things when she so desperately needed them to fall into place? She hadn't expected it to happen by some miracle or another. She expected hard work, but she had also expected that her hard work would show results. So far, all she had managed was heartbreak.

She didn't understand it. It didn't make sense.

"Why would God make me feel this way if it's not what He has planned for me?" she wailed.

Sarah Ann pulled away, her gaze searching Evie's face, but her sister didn't speak. Evie had the feeling she didn't want to say what was on her mind. It didn't take a fancy *Englisch* education to figure out what was going on in that pretty head. She didn't think Evie was right. She didn't want her to move out on her own. Maybe all these mistakes were really God's way of telling her she needed to stay right where she was.

"No." She shook her head and wrenched out of her sister's embrace. "There is a way. I'm just not seeing it."

There has to be.

But how?

Or was she completely wrong in her thinking about God's plan for her?

"For I know the plans I have for you," declares the Lord.

Were His plans the same as hers?

"It's okay, Evie," Sarah Ann said.

Evie shook her head. "It's not okay. I have dreams and I deserve to live them." She felt that way straight to her bones, even as she realized what a selfish statement it was. She should be living for God. And she was. With a side of independence and goat milk soap.

"Maybe—" Sarah Ann didn't finish.

Evie didn't have to hear the words to know what she was going to say.

Maybe you just need some help.

Evie met her sister's concerned gaze, her own filled with determination. She hoped anyway. "I'm going to do this," she said. "Somehow, someway, I will do this."

Saturday Evie finally made soap, but she wasn't happy with the amount she got out of the work she was doing. Milking the goats, making the soap, waiting for it to dry and then dressing it up to appeal to the *Englischers* who would most likely be her customers. It didn't quite seem worth it at the end of the day. Even without disasters and twenty-six goats of her own. The joy of her accomplishment was over-shadowed by the sheer exhaustion of the work she had to put into it.

She slept so hard Saturday night that she snoozed through her alarm Sunday morning. Naomi finally woke her up, and she had to rush around in order to make it to church on time.

Now she was nibbling on a piece of cheese as the youth group had gathered in the barn for the evening's singing.

She allowed her gaze to roam around the area, noting with a surge of joy that Freeman was across the room, staring back at her. She swallowed the bite she had in her mouth and gave him a small smile. She was happy to see him there. Somehow, she had missed him be-fore church and afterward at the meal. She had been busy serving food, and he had been busy putting up the church benches, and all of a sud-den it was time to go home and milk the goats.

She had wanted to talk to him so badly. It had been days since she had talked to him, though it seemed like forever. Here was her chance.

Evie stuffed the rest of the piece of cheese into her mouth and made her way across to where Freeman waited.

With her mouth full, she couldn't even say hi, but they were close. Did it really matter? Maybe not, after the way she had talked to him the last time they were together.

Without a word, he handed her a cup of lemonade. Not his, but a second one he held. Perhaps he had been on his way to talk to her when she was on her way to talk to him?

Evie gratefully took his offering and washed down the cheese. "Thank you," she said with a smile.

"You're welcome," he replied.

A normal exchange, but did it somehow feel more…intimate? Or was she simply imagining things?

She stared up into his sweet brown eyes, seeing things there she couldn't decipher.

Across the room the others gathered on the benches and prepared to sing.

"Are you ready for this?" he asked her.

She looked at the group of them all laughing and talking amongst themselves as they settled in for singing. "No," she whispered.

He barely heard her, but the word was there, hanging between them like a thread of hope. But he was getting ahead of himself.

"You don't want to sing?" he asked.

She shook her head. "I think I want to go somewhere and talk."

His heart couldn't have soared any higher. She wanted to go somewhere and talk. She had already told him *no* in a dozen different ways, in front of people, alone, wherever they happened to be. But now she wanted to talk privately. Surely that had to mean something.

"I could drive you home," he offered. His voice still had that unused quality, and he resisted the urge to clear his throat.

"Jah." She gave a jerky nod as if she was as nervous as he.

"Okay," he replied. "Give me a minute."

Freeman could feel all eyes on him as he made his way over to his sister Rebecca to tell her what was going on. He had brought Claire tonight, and if he was leaving now, she would need to get a ride home from Rebecca.

Once the issues with his sisters were straightened out, he was back at Evie's side in a flash. This was it. Somehow, he could feel it. Tonight was the night.

Chapter Thirteen

Evie's palms were so sweaty she could barely keep her hands on the grips of her crutches. She could do this though. She needed to.

After talking with Sarah Ann the day before, Evie had come to a few realizations. She had been telling her sister that a change in plans was sometimes necessary, even when you might not think that was what you wanted. Sometimes what you thought you wanted and what God had planned for you were two very different things. You had to be open to change and shifts and all sorts of other curves in order to live your best life, as they say. She liked to add *for the Lord*. To live your best life *for the Lord*.

Perhaps Evie herself wasn't accepting the curves and setbacks for what they were, signs that maybe she was heading in the wrong direction. Even after reluctantly donning her spectacles and reading over the recipe and remaking the soap and having it actually come out as a usable product, somehow it seemed less satisfying than she had anticipated. Why was that?

She had no idea, but Sarah Ann had told her that maybe she wasn't supposed to be making soaps. Maybe, she wasn't supposed to be milking goats, raising the beasts. And maybe, just maybe, she wasn't supposed to be trying to stamp her independence so untiringly on her life.

What was wrong with a partnership? A marriage? A helpmate? It didn't have anything to do with her disabilities. It was as God had set forth in the Bible in Corinthians.

Nevertheless neither is the man without the woman, neither the woman without the man, in the Lord.

It wasn't right for the two of them to be alone. Not when they could be together. It was so simple and yet it was the answer that she had refused to see.

Okay, maybe not so simple. Evie was nervous beyond belief. How could she talk to Freeman about love? If he would love her enough if she agreed to marry him. If he could truly forget all about Helen Schrock. Was such a thing even possible?

Evie's mouth was dry and her throat scratchy as she pulled herself into his buggy. He hadn't said a word as they walked out of the barn and into the night. Now they were all alone. There was no one around to hear them talk, overhear their secrets, barge in with their own opinions. Just the two of them.

"I feel like I should say something, but then I feel like you have something you need to say."

"I do," she managed to croak out. She sounded like she had swallowed that big ol' bullfrog that lived out in the pond behind her *mammi*'s *haus*.

The truth was, Freeman didn't sound much better. Too much emotion was clogging their airways and making it hard to get out what needed to be said.

Lord, give me strength, she silently prayed. *Amen.*

"I've been giving it some thought," she started, unsure if where she was headed was the right place to begin. "I've been dreaming of living all by myself and proving that I can make a living and pay my bills so that I don't need anyone else to help me."

He made a noise beside her but didn't take his gaze from the dark road. It was hard to see going up and down the small hills that littered the valley, around the curves and such. Even with the headlights shining the way, it was sometimes difficult to tell where you were on the road as you drove along.

Though she had a feeling his lack of eye contact had to do with his own overflowing emotions.

Something had definitely happened between them in the weeks since Helen had been gone. It was as if she had been some force keeping them from each other whether she meant to or not, throwing everything into some kind of orbit but never letting them connect. However, now that she was gone…

"We know that God tells us that's not the plan He has for us. He made us for one another, one to help the other and the other to help the one. But I wasn't looking at it like that."

Suddenly Freeman pulled the buggy to the side of the road, which could be dangerous, but when she looked around, she saw that they were in the parking lot for the cemetery.

At least they were safe.

He stopped the horse completely, then turned in his seat to look at her full in the face. "Evie, what are you trying to say?"

She sucked in a deep breath and expelled it

slowly while he waited, his eyes blazing in the artificial glow given off by the security lights.

"I love you." Her voice was breathless and wispy, almost nonexistent as she shared her deepest secret. "I love you and I always have. And you've always loved Helen, and now she's gone, and you say you love me. But how do I know that if she comes back that you will still love me? That you won't regret your proposal." The words all ran together in her haste to get them out before she chickened out.

He stared at her for a full minute before blinking hard, as if that would somehow help him arrange her words into something that he could understand.

"You love me?" He repeated the words slowly, as if he were speaking a language he had never spoken before. "You say you always have. Are you talking as a friend?"

He just had to have her say it outright. A small, cynical laugh escaped her. She hated the sound of it. It didn't belong there in their beautiful night. "No. As more than a friend." Again, her voice was tiny and unsubstantial. "Always as more than a friend." She stiffened her spine in order to continue. "And I'm afraid that if I agree to marry you—even though I want to say yes so badly—that one day you will regret your

decision. Someday when I can't uphold my end
of the bargain. I worry about how I'm going
to take care of a passel of kids all by myself
while you are working. And what happens if
I get hurt or can't do something? What then?"

She didn't finish and say the rest. That she
couldn't do the things that able-bodied Helen
could. And she didn't want him to regret his
decision. She couldn't stomach that at all.

He shook his head, as if the words were beyond his comprehension. Or perhaps he was
looking for a way to let her down easy. She
should have kept it all to herself. "Never mind."
She was so stupid.

"How come you're just now bringing this up?
I mean, I don't view you that way."

Because that was not what she wanted the
world to see of her. She wanted to be the strong
one, the dependable one, the stable one. She
wasn't sure why those values were so important to her, they just were. Now it felt like they
might have hurt her a little as well. "I do everything in my power so that people don't see
me like that."

"You don't like asking for help," he said
knowingly.

"No," she said. "I don't. All my life I've felt
weak and behind, inferior—"

He placed a finger over her lips to stop the flow of her words. "Don't say that about yourself. We all need help."

The touch was small and electric, tingling all through her as she sat there and waited for him to move away. He stayed close but pulled his hand back.

Everyone needed help. But she needed more than most. And she hated it. But with some time maybe Freeman could help her get over that. But only if he could love her in return.

"That's it?" he asked her, his voice thin and reedy.

His proximity, though it unnerved her, gave her strength as well. Strength to continue.

She nodded.

"Evie, that's the craziest thing I've ever heard. That's why we have each other. Not only husband and wife, but families. To lean on each other when times get tough. No man is an island."

She stared at him, his words prickling her like frozen pellets in an ice storm. But his look wasn't cold. It was warm, inviting, caring. "Is that in the Bible?"

He chuckled and shook his head. "No. It's a poem I read a long time ago. It has stuck with me all these years because of how true it is.

The man who wrote it was an *Englischer*, but it's how we live. He understood that. We can't be completely separate, because we need each other."

"It sounds like something Jesus might have said." She had been wondering how she missed it.

"You're right about that," Freeman agreed.

She felt the heat rise all the way up to her hairline and past the new prayer *kapp* she'd had made the day before. She could hardly believe that she was having this conversation with him.

Her stomach clenched as he continued.

"You love me and think that I'll go back to loving Helen?"

She nodded, tears pushing against her will to keep them back. They won and raced down her cheeks.

"I've always loved you too. I just couldn't see it when Helen was around. Now I do. You're the kindest, smartest person I know. You can sew up a storm, you work hard, and you always have a smile for whoever is standing next to you. But that's not why I love you. I love you because I love you and no other reason. But to make you feel better, we won't get married right away. I mean, that's what I wanted. But I can wait. I can give you time to become set-

tled to the fact that it's you and only you whom
I love."

"You will?"

"*Jah*, of course. And children? We'll figure
that out when the time comes. But neither will
happen until you say you'll marry me. Now,
Evie Ebersol…will you marry me?"

Her tears kept coming. *"Jah,"* she whispered
into the crisp night air. Then she leaned over
in her seat and pressed her lips to his.

She was going to marry Freeman Yoder.

Monday dawned with Evie having only one
regret. That she had kissed Freeman the night
before. It wasn't like her to be so forward, yet
how could she be sorry for the zing that shot
through her like lightning across the nighttime
sky? He kissed her back, only briefly, then they
broke apart, still a little emotional from the
conversation they'd just had.

Freeman had dropped her off at Mattie's with
the promise that he would see her the following
day. She had practically floated into her room,
if that were even possible, and slept like a baby,
dreaming of weddings and organic farms and
rainbows and happiness. Maybe there was
something to being open and honest with each
other. And he hadn't said one word about that

silly childhood promise he had made to her so many years ago. They had a new promise now.

Evie rose from her bed and dressed for the day, taking extra care with her appearance. Freeman was coming to see her later. She didn't have to go out and milk the goats, or worry about soap making, though she would have to take the books back to the library that week and explain what happened to the one she'd gotten soap all over. Perhaps they wouldn't make her pay for the damages, and instead slip a note into the pages with a warning about what happens when the directions aren't followed.

"Someone looks happy," Naomi said as she came into the kitchen just in time to help put the finishing touches on breakfast.

Evie's smile deepened. She couldn't help it. She had been worried for so long about this, she hadn't even realized the weight it had given her until it had been lifted. She and Freeman Yoder were engaged to be married. It would be a while before they actually said their vows, but she would be his helpmate all the same. She would work on his farm, perhaps find her own job and share it with him. Then everything would be absolutely golden.

"This doesn't have anything to do with Freeman, does it?" Mattie asked with a flippant look in her direction. She slid the pancake onto the waiting plate with the ease of a professional chef.

"Maybe." Evie was about to burst with the news. She wanted to tell her sisters so badly. But she and Freeman agreed to wait a bit before sharing their news with the world. So that was all she would say. For now. Besides, her sisters were smart. They knew the truth without her saying a word on the matter.

They all sat down to breakfast and ate, the atmosphere happy and lively like it always was at Mattie's house. Soon it would be even more lively when she and Samuel married. Naomi might stay on to help with the girls or maybe move back in with their *dat*. Surely by then, Evie would be living—

Heavens! She needed to call Judy and tell her about the change of plans. She hoped the woman wasn't too unhappy with the news. Evie liked Judy a lot, and she didn't want to upset the woman. Who knew when their paths might cross again?

Anyway, perhaps by the time Samuel and Mattie married, Evie and Freeman would be married as well. Just the thought made Evie sigh with happiness.

Once the girls were cleaned and dressed and the breakfast dishes washed and put away, Evie headed over to the phone shanty to call Judy. It was a short walk and normally she dreaded it. Today was a beautiful day.

Truthfully, it was a little overcast with the sun fighting the clouds for dominance over the sky. Whatever the weather, it was still a beautiful day. She loved Freeman and he loved her and soon they would tell everyone, and they would get married and all would be right in the world. How she imagined it when she was a little girl. Before she realized that some dreams might have to be put aside.

Now she knew those dreams might be attainable, and she shared those dreams with him. They would sort them out and make them come true together. What more could a person ask for?

She arrived at the phone shanty with a message pinned to the wall for her to call Judy. Even though it was a written note, it seemed urgent in its lettering. ASAP was underlined twice.

She picked up the receiver and dialed the familiar number.

"Evie, thank goodness it's you." Judy seemed harried and distraught.

"*Jah*, Judy. It's me. What's wrong? You sound upset."

"Oh, dear," she said. Evie could almost see the woman wringing her hands on the other end of the line. "My cousin was just released from the hospital. I didn't even know he had been injured. He had to have surgery and had to have a leg amputated. He needs a place to stay and recover where he can have some independence and still be close to someone if he needs help. The family got together and decided my little guesthouse would be the perfect place for him to convalesce."

"Oh." Evie wasn't sure what to say to all that. "I'm glad he's doing all right. God is good."

"You are a sweetheart, you know that? I'm so sorry that I can't uphold my promise to you, but he's family. I have no idea how long he'll be here. Everything is up in the air."

"It's all right, Judy."

The woman grew quiet. "Is everything okay, dear?"

Evie smiled even though she knew Judy couldn't see it. She couldn't help it; she was that happy. "Well, I'm getting married."

"Oh! Oh, my, that is such good news!"

"Jah," Evie said. "It certainly is."

"Well, then," Judy continued. "I'm so happy it all worked out for the both of us."

"Me too," Evie said, that smile still shining

on her face. She said her goodbyes to Judy and headed back to the house. Just as she got to the driveway, she saw a familiar yellow buggy headed her way.

She waited until he got even with her, but the look on his face would have stopped her in her tracks.

"What's wrong?" Surely not one of his siblings. The look Freeman held was grim.

"Climb in," he said and waited patiently for her to comply.

"What is it?" she asked again, but he shook his head.

"Let's wait until we can really talk about this."

If the look on his face wasn't enough, his tone was terrifying.

She held her questions until he parked the buggy in front of Mattie's house.

Freeman climbed down, then came around to help Evie. For once she didn't protest at the assistance. Something about his demeanor lent an urgency to everything.

The sun had gone behind the clouds once more, the sky matching the gloom on his face.

"Are you going to tell me now?" she asked.

He motioned to the front porch, then waited patiently for her to climb the steps and settle down in one of the rocking chairs that Mattie kept there. Freeman perched on the edge of the other, as if he might need to spring up at any moment. For what, she had no idea. He reached over and took her hands into his own.

"Evie." He stopped, sucked in a deep breath as if to fortify his resolve, then continued. "I love you. I proposed to you and I'm going to marry you," he said. "So, I had to come by and tell you. To let you be the first to know from me."

She hated the frown that marred his brow, the slight tremor in his hands as they held hers. "What is it?"

"Helen's come home from Lancaster."

Chapter Fourteen

The entire community was abuzz with news. Helen had returned. Before Evie had even a moment to tell her family, to bask in the joy of her good news, speculation had started. Had Helen returned to marry Freeman and restore everything back to the world as everyone knew it?

Freeman had already stated his intentions. He was going to marry Evie, and she needed to ignore all the speculation and gossip. It was no easy feat, but she was giving it her best.

The day after Helen returned, she came to visit Evie and tell her all about Lancaster, the buggies, the shops, the iconic stores and eateries that people—*Englisch* and Amish alike— had to visit if they had the opportunity to visit Lancaster County. Evie had listened and absorbed all the fancy details that Helen described.

"Is something wrong?" Helen had asked.

Truthfully, Evie was wondering the same thing of Helen, but she hadn't asked. Evie hadn't left Millers Creek. Everything in her life was presumably the same. Helen on the other hand had just returned from an extended trip to Lancaster County after breaking up with her longtime beau. Of course she had changed. It was inevitable.

"Of course not," Evie had answered, respecting Freeman's request that they hold off announcing their news until things had settled down. Evie was fine with the decision, but it was hard keeping her sweet secret to herself.

The hardest part of the first few days after Helen's return was that Evie wasn't able to see as much of Freeman. Some of it had to do with the work he still had to complete at his farm and house. Evie desperately wanted to help him as she had promised, but he thought it best to wait and not raise anyone's suspicions more than they already were. Another part of it was it seemed as if Helen coming back had put a strain on the time they once had.

Helen appeared to be everywhere at once, flitting back and forth between the two of them as if somehow she knew that something was going on. Yet that was a secret they weren't ready to share. Soon, Freeman had promised.

Then, after Helen had been in town for a week, she came for another visit and said, "Can I talk to you, Evie?"

Helen being back was the week's biggest news, including all the tales from her trip and her promises that she had come home to Millers Creek to stay. The week had also included one buddy bunch Thursday get-together. Evie had begged off from attending, stating that Mattie needed her to help with something at the house that couldn't wait until another time.

Now it was the Friday after and Helen was wringing her hands and needing to talk about something.

"Sure," Evie said, pushing an irritated and protesting Charlie back into the house with one crutch before stepping out onto the porch and shutting the front door behind her. "What's up?"

"Well…" Helen moved to sit in one of the rocking chairs there on Mattie's front porch, and the thought ran through Evie's head that she couldn't wait to have visitors on *her* front porch. Hers and Freeman's.

Evie settled across from her and waited for her friend to continue.

"Last night was the buddy bunch get-together."

Evie nodded encouragingly.

Helen shook her head as if trying to shuffle her thoughts around and get them back in the correct order. "I don't know how to explain it," she finally said. "I could just tell that something was off."

"How so?" Why was Helen asking her? Evie hadn't even been there the night before.

"I felt like everyone was staring at me. Like I had forgotten my prayer covering or something."

"Had you?" Evie asked.

"Of course not," Helen retorted. "It only felt that way."

"I see." Evie gave a stiff nod. "Maybe it was you coming back and all. You know, everyone wondering about your trip."

"I suppose." Helen dropped her gaze and began pleating little folds into the fabric of her apron. The material was different, a little pattern sewn into the fabric so small that a person had to be right up on it to see it. A Lancaster legacy, Evie was certain.

"Why do I feel like there's more?" Evie finally asked.

Helen drew in a deep breath and let it out on a long, shuddering sigh. "Do you think Freeman started seeing someone else while I was gone?"

Evie drew back a bit but managed to stop herself from pulling completely away from her friend. "You were only gone for a few weeks," she stuttered, only vaguely realizing that she hadn't answered Helen's question at all.

"I don't know." Helen gave a delicate shrug. "I told you it was hard to describe, but it felt like everyone was in on a secret about me."

"That's...that's ridiculous," Evie managed. No one else knew about her and Freeman, at least not with 100 percent certainty. That had to be what Helen was sensing. Evie was doubly glad that she had decided not to attend the event. That would have only made matters worse. She was so bad at deception. That should be a good quality to have, but when faced with such upheaval that needed to be sorted through before the truth could be shared, it was more of a hindrance.

"I thought so too." She sniffed and looked off into the distance as if something even heavier was weighing on her mind.

"Helen?" Evie questioned after several minutes of Helen looking away, not saying a word.

Her friend stirred and shifted in her seat as if she had been unaware of her actions the entire time.

"I thought he would wait on me, you know.

That he would be here when I got back and now I—" She shook her head. "I suppose I made a mistake." She let out a choked laugh. "More than one. Maybe even more than my fair share. Then I thought I would return home, and I could put everything back where it was before."

Just like the two of them, like she and Freeman, had suspected. Then everything changed when Freeman remembered that silly, silly promise he had made to her so long ago. He swore that his feelings now didn't have anything to do with that promise and she believed him. Neither did hers. And now...

Now everything was different and messed up and in complete upheaval.

"That sounds so naive to say it now, but I guess I was hopeful," Helen continued.

Evie reached out and squeezed Helen's fingers, doing her best to reassure her friend without deceiving her further, but she knew it was impossible to curb her untruthfulness. Her tales of half-truths. "I'm sure it will be all right." Surely that would hold true. It would all turn out eventually. It might not turn out the way any of them wanted, but it would turn out. They simply had to hold steady and trust God.

Helen picked up Evie's hand. Tears sprang into her deep, ocean-blue eyes as she lovingly squeezed Evie's fingers in return. Friends to the end. "I hope you're right, Evie. I surely hope and pray that you are right."

Freeman pushed the chair to the other side of the porch and stood back to look at it. What he really wanted was a swing to go on this end of the house. A swing where he could sit with Evie as the sun went down and talk about children. And life and love and everything beautiful under the sun. But that would have to wait.

He had hoped that they would be able to talk to the bishop before the end of the summer about getting married the following fall. He wanted to marry her as soon as he could after the harvest. He had already looked at a calendar, and the second of November was a Tuesday. It seemed perfect to him. As perfect as could be. Though now that Helen was back, the whole idea of marrying Evie was surreal, as if the past few weeks had been part of some incredibly real dream he had, and now he was awake and struggling to remember what had really happened and what he had imagined.

The thing was, he didn't want to have to imagine what was real. He wanted his time with Evie to be his truth. It *was* his truth, and he had to hold on to that.

It didn't help that everyone had been staring at the two of them—him and Helen—at the last get-together their buddy bunch had held on Thursday night. And at church on Sunday. Normally he and Helen and Evie would all get clustered together to discuss one thing or another, but as soon as the service let out, Evie was nowhere to be seen. Helen had claimed all his attention, and once again everyone was speculating.

That evening he had begged off going to the singing but had managed not to run straight over and make sure Evie was all right. They had to have a little space right now until they could work through the situation with Helen.

It was the next thing on his list of to-dos for the day.

1. Set up the porch furniture
2. Clean through the shed
3. Go over and talk to Helen

After that, it was anyone's guess what he needed to do. He couldn't think past going to talk to Helen, clearing the air with her and stating his intentions to marry Evie. He was afraid that the discussion would take a while. He and Helen had been talking about getting married for as long as either one of them had even known what a marriage was. But now… they wanted different things. He knew it. It was apparent to him, as clear as the nose on his face. He had to make sure that Helen could see it too. The last thing he wanted to do was hurt her. However, he was confident that once he explained it to her, she would be able to see the truth as well. He had to proceed with caution and care and loving concern. After all, they had always been the best of friends, and he cherished that relationship even more than a romantic one.

Satisfied with the look of the porch for the time being, he started around the side of the house to the outbuildings William Hostetler had built to house his wagons, buggies and other farming equipment. When he had moved, he had sold everything to Freeman with the exception of the household goods they would need to set up in the *dawdihaus* attached to his son's place in Indiana. Freeman was still digging through the storage shed finding long-forgotten treasures that seemed as bright and new as a shiny penny to him.

He had just uncovered a plastic tub under a tarp and was dragging it out into the sun to see what was inside when a familiar voice sounded behind him.

"There you are."

He straightened and whirled around, automatically brushing the dust from his pants as he did so. He was covered in dirt and had already decided that he would have to change before he went to Helen's to talk with her about everything that had happened while she was away. Now she was standing in his backyard as fresh and lovely as she always appeared.

"Helen," he gasped, still brushing bits of old leaves and cobwebs from his clothing before smiling up at her.

Her face lit in return, and he noted once again how beautiful she was. It was almost distracting, a fact that he had never noticed until she left and came back. Odd. Why wouldn't he have noticed it before?

Why did you never notice how wrong you are for each other and how compatible you and Evie seem to be?

"Hi, Freeman. I hope I'm not interrupting anything."

It was obvious that she had, but he wasn't about to point that out. "No. No. Of course not. I was just about to head over to your place."

She shot a pointed look at the streaks of dust

and grime on his broadfall pants. That was one thing he did not always enjoy when it came to Helen. She was definitely a neatnik. He believed in cleanliness, wholeheartedly. But hard work required a body to get a little—and even a lot—dirty from time to time. When that time came he embraced it and washed up when it was over. Helen preferred to stay mess-free all day long. "I see."

"I was going to change beforehand," he replied, hating the defensive tone his voice had taken on. He didn't like it one bit. "I'm going to clean out this shed first." He glanced back over his shoulder at the piled-to-the-rafters space behind him. "Well, part of it anyway."

"But now I'm here," she said.

"Now you're here." He dusted his hands as if brushing off the awkward feelings rising between them. Their relationship had never been so strange until now. Until this. He didn't know what to do about it. Now that she was home, he wanted his friend back. He was a little anxious that Helen might have a hard time when he told her that he was going to marry Evie, but he felt certain after a while everything would return to normal. He hoped anyway.

"Can we go inside and talk?" She gestured back over her shoulder toward the house.

"Jah." He brushed his hands once again, this time on the seat of his pants, and gestured for her to lead the way toward the back door of his new farmhouse.

"I was surprised to learn that you went ahead and bought this place," Helen said as she perched on one of the dining chairs in the kitchen. He had a small table there where he had been eating his meals. There was no sense in having anything bigger since it was only him. He made his way to the kitchen sink and started scrubbing his hands.

"Jah," he said over his shoulder as he dried his hands. "I figured it was an investment into my future." His future. Not theirs. She didn't miss his choice of words. He could tell when she opened her eyes a little bit wider in surprise. She recovered well and smiled sweetly as he sat down across from her.

Now that he was closer and able to see her every nuance and expression he noticed that her eyes were red-rimmed, her nose a little bit pink as if she was coming down with something.

"You okay?" he asked, watching closely for her reaction. He had expected her maybe to say that she was getting a cold or that her hay fever had kicked in a little earlier this year.

Instead, her eyes filled with tears, fat tears that ran down her cheeks in twin rivers of sadness.

"H-Helen," he started, not knowing what he said. Not knowing what to do to make it better. He hated when a woman cried. All the women he knew were tough as nails. They pulled their weight and worked side by side with the men in their lives, be it their husbands, brothers or fathers. They could all hold their own. This was something he didn't understand. At all. "What—?"

He didn't get to finish; she was out of her chair in a heartbeat, her prayer *kapp* strings trailing behind her as she threw herself to the floor at his feet. She wrapped her arms around his knees and tilted her head up to look at him, tears still falling. Then she laid her cheek against his knee and sobbed.

"Helen," he started again, softly this time. "What's wrong?" He laid a comforting, though awkward, hand on her shoulder.

She held on tighter and seemed to cry even harder at his gentle touch.

"Oh, Helen. I can't help you if you don't tell me what's wrong." He got a little more comfortable with having her so close, arms wrapped around his legs. He just wished she wasn't sit-

ting on the floor. Yet he knew if he lifted her
to her feet, that she would merely collapse into
his lap. And that would never do.

He waited a heartbeat more. Then another.
And another. He had decided to try and disen-
gage her from his legs and see if he could get
her to talk about it—whatever *it* was—when
she finally started pulling herself together.

She sat up, lifting her head, holding on to
him as if she were afraid to let him go. She
wiped her eyes against the sleeves of her dress
in an effort to dispense her tears. The only
problem was more followed shortly after. It
was as if her eyes had sprung a leak.

He waited until she took a deep shuddering
breath before smoothing the back of his fingers against her soft, damp cheek. "How about
a glass of water?" he offered. He wanted to
know what was causing her such grief, but he
figured she needed a moment or two more to
pull herself together enough to share whatever
was vexing her so.

Finally, she released his legs then sniffed.
He stood and made his way to the sink. Behind
him, he heard her push to her feet as he took
a glass from the cabinet and drew her a cup of
water from the tap.

When he returned to the table with her drink,

she was once again seated across from where he had been sitting. He pushed the glass into her waiting hands, then returned to his seat.

"When you're ready," he said, giving her a quick nod as she swallowed a pull of the water and set the glass on the table between them.

She shook her head, and her eyes filled with tears, but this time she managed to control them. "Oh, Freeman, I messed up. I really messed everything up."

Was this about Evie? Had she found out that he and Evie were making secret plans to be married come fall of the following year? Was Helen now realizing that she had messed up by leaving him behind for Evie to scoop up?

Even as the idea went through his head, he realized how ridiculous it sounded. He wasn't some prize to be won or lost. Helen wouldn't think leaving him was the biggest mistake she had ever made. It went beyond his scope of reason.

"How so?" he finally asked her, certain that whatever it was couldn't be as bad as she was making it seem.

She closed her eyes for a moment, then opened them once again. Her lips trembled as she spoke. "I'm going to have a baby."

Chapter Fifteen

He finally knew what a person meant when they said, *You could have knocked me over with a feather.* He wasn't sure it would even take all that to put him on the floor after she said those fateful words. He was glad he was sitting down already. If not, he would have surely fallen straight to the ground.

"What?" The word barely made it out of his mouth and into the world. He was surprised it didn't get stuck behind the knot forming in his throat.

"Please don't make me say it again." Her tears started back up, and he rose to his feet, snatching up a couple of paper towels from the roll sitting on the counter. Not the best to dry tears, but they were close at hand.

She gratefully accepted the bundle of paper towels and dried her face. She blew her nose delicately, then wadded up the makeshift tissue and placed it on the table near her elbow.

"The, uh, father?" Freeman could barely get the words out, though it was the most logical question to come next.

Helen let out a derisive, self-mocking laugh and dabbed at the tears that had started once again. "It doesn't matter," she finally said. "He doesn't matter."

Freeman took a moment to gather his thoughts. Her answer was cryptic and telling. She didn't want to say who the father was. Most likely he was someone she had met while she was away in Lancaster. Freeman guessed anyway. He couldn't imagine her doing something like that while still dating him. Though he supposed that it was possible, it seemed more likely that Helen got swept up in the glitz of Lancaster and had fallen into the trap of desire. One thing was certain: there was more to the story than she was willing to tell, but it was her story after all. Yet he wondered: was the man Amish or *Englisch*? "What are you going to do?"

Her lips pressed together as she once again wagged her head sadly from side to side. "I don't really know," she whispered.

"Have you talked to your parents?"

"No." The word was quiet and loaded with meaning. How would her parents take such news? Not well. That much was certain. But they would help her as soon as she went in front of the church and confessed her sins. It would be hard, and her life would be forever changed.

Theirs wasn't the most conservative community in the valley, but they were still Old Order and very conservative by most outsider's standards. Having a baby and not being married—

Something in him clicked. Suddenly he knew why she had come to him first.

"Have you told anyone else?" he asked as he sank back into his chair.

She shook her head once more and reached across the table toward him. "You're all I have, Freeman."

"So, you came here." He didn't want this to be pushed on him. He wanted to marry Evie, start a family with her. Not marry Helen to help her save face.

"Everyone's going to think it's yours anyway. I thought—"

He held up a hand. He didn't want to hear her reasoning. He didn't need to hear it. She was right that everyone would automatically assume that the baby was his. Yet to stand up and pretend that it was seemed as much of a sin. But could he allow his friend to suffer the fate that her mistake was dragging her toward?

No. That was the long and the short of it. But what would Evie say? What would she do when he told her that Helen was pregnant?

"Forget I said anything."

He jerked his attention toward Helen as she stood so quickly, she almost knocked her chair to the floor. "I shouldn't have come here. I shouldn't have asked this of you."

"Who else would you have asked it of?" he demanded. He hadn't meant to sound so harsh, but the words were already out there, and he couldn't take them back. He knew she was hurting, but he was as well. Life as he had known it was about to change. Forever. There would be no getting it back to the way it was before.

"Sit down, Helen." He used a gentler tone this time, and she complied, perching on the edge of her seat as if she would be bolting at any second.

"I'm sorry," she whispered. "I just thought—"

She thought that because he had been smitten with her when she left that he would be as smitten with her when she returned. Perhaps even enough to marry her for the sake of a child that wasn't his.

This isn't about you.

The voice in his head was clear and firm.

It wasn't about him. It was about a baby, and a best friend who would have to bear a burden most couldn't carry.

What about Evie?

She was his friend as well, and even more than that, he loved her. She would be hurt when he broke it off with her, though not as hurt for as long as an innocent child and a beautiful woman who got caught up in the thrill and made an irreversible mistake.

"Who's the father?" he asked once more, leaving all the accusation from his words.

"He's an *Englisch* man I met in Lancaster at a party. I don't know who he was. I only knew him by his nickname. They called him Dutch."

Her story didn't add up. It was one thing for a young Amish woman to give in to those temptations with the man she was soon to marry, but to a stranger? To someone she didn't even know by name? There was something suspicious about the entire thing. He couldn't expect her to give up all her secrets at one time.

"He's *Englisch* though." It was part statement, part question. The most important fact that she could give him. She couldn't leave their community. He knew that now, and if she didn't find someone who would marry her she would remain on the fringes of their community. If the father came to her she would be expected to marry him, be he *Englisch* or Amish. Her *mamm* would be heartbroken.

"Jah," she said. "I started hanging out with the wrong people, I suppose."

That could happen to anyone. That was why the church preached about staying near, not straying and resisting the temptations of the world. Even during *rumspringa*. It was a slippery slope from where they lived into a pit of sin.

"I'm going to need a little time," he told her.

"I understand." She nodded. "The woman you've been seeing while I was away."

He stopped, his heart in his throat. "How did you know about that?"

"It's a small community." She shrugged and flashed a sad, quick smile his way. "Will she understand?"

Would she? He had no idea. But he would soon find out.

"I don't know," he said honestly. "Does it matter either way?"

Helen didn't answer. She didn't have to. It didn't matter because this was bigger than Evie or him or even Helen. This was about an innocent little baby who had no say in the matter at all.

* * *

Evie rushed out onto the porch, dragging Charlie with her on a length of rope. Normally the goat wanted outside at all costs. All costs except being tied to the porch support post, even if on a twenty-five-foot lead.

"Come on." Evie tugged at the stubborn goat, needing the chore complete before Freeman arrived.

He had called the shanty phone the day before to tell her that he had something to talk to her about and that he would be over the following day after lunch.

Now it was after noon, and she was anxious for him to arrive. Mostly because she hadn't seen him much since Helen had come back to town, but a little bit because he had never called the shanty the day before a visit to let her know he was coming over. Like everyone else in their community, he hopped in his buggy and buzzed over when the need suited him.

That alone made this meeting…special, made her wonder what Freeman had on his mind. As if she had produced him by imagining him, she caught sight of his yellow buggy coming up the drive as she finished the last knot to secure Charlie to the support post.

The goat bleated at her in protest as if she

knew that in her spare time Evie had ridden into town to the library and found a book on tying knots in order to keep Charlie contained at the end of a rope.

"Now behave yourself," she told the goat. Sometimes the animal was worse than a child. Kid was an apt name for baby goats. It was as if whoever came up with the term had a goat of their own. Never mind that Charlie was full-grown. She was definitely a "kid at heart."

Evie smiled at her own joke, pleased with herself for making sure the animal stayed put and that Freeman was on his way to the house. She climbed the stairs and waited for him to draw near.

She was still smiling when he hopped down from the buggy, but there was something in the set of his shoulders that made her smile straighten and her heart flutter with worry.

Something had happened. Something bad. Or at the very least, not good.

"Freeman?" she called to him.

He looked up at her and smiled, but the action didn't reach his eyes.

"I don't understand," Naomi said again with a shake of her head. The sisters had all gathered in Evie's room as she cried and packed up her stuff to leave and go back to her father's house.

"He said he couldn't marry me after all. He was in love with Helen. He always had been. He was going to marry her like they had always planned. Maybe even sooner."

Naomi stopped pacing the room and swung back to Evie. "Oh, honey…"

Evie wiped away the tears with one hand, then went back to packing her bag.

"I don't understand why you think you have to go back home," Mattie said from her place on the side of the bed.

"I'm going to have to sooner or later." Her little place at the edge of town was gone. This fall, Samuel and Mattie would get married, and they wouldn't want *two* sisters there helping out with the baby. They might not even want one, which meant Naomi would be packing up too. Evie knew one thing: two was definitely too many, and she needed to get back to the life she knew she would be living—at home, unmarried, taking care of her father. She wouldn't even have to move him out into the *dawdihaus*. What difference would it make if there was only the two of them living there?

Evie saw her sisters share a look, and she did her best to ignore it. It really hurt too much to talk about it. She had thought she had found the one. The one man who understood her. Who accepted her for who she was, accepted her for *how* she was. Yet she had been wrong about that. In so many ways. She had been caught up in the magic that was Freeman, his sweet ways and his belief in the stupid promise of a six-year-old boy. She had been thunderstruck, staggered and stunned, that he felt the same for her as she had for him. Then the bottom fell out of it all.

There was a part of her that wanted Helen to go away again, that wished she had never come back at all, but Helen had been her friend for as long as Evie could remember. She should be glad her friend was back, not battling her for the affections of a man who didn't want her. So, Evie was letting it go. Letting him go. It was the easiest way. Well, no way was *easy*. Still, it was better to not fight. Better to accept that he didn't really love her, despite the kiss they shared and the times they had spent together since Helen left. She needed to chalk it up to a learning experience. Girls like her weren't really allowed to have such dreams. Evie was twenty-six and she couldn't do everything she wanted to do. She had to have help. It was a fact of life she needed to face up to and quickly.

There was no getting around it, no changing it. It simply was. Like the fact that Freeman was going to marry Helen.

"You don't have to leave," Mattie said once more.

"I've already talked to Dat," Evie told them. "He's going to build me some covered dog kennels in the backyard where I can raise those little bitty dogs the *Englischers* like to carry around in their purses."

"Chihuahuas?" Naomi asked, pulling a face to show what she thought of the idea.

"No, the cuter ones. From England."

"Yorkshire terriers?" Mattie asked.

Evie pointed to Mattie. "That's the one."

"What do you know about Yorkies?" Naomi demanded. "You couldn't even remember their breed's name."

"What does anybody know about anything?" she asked cryptically. "Until you learn."

Mattie laid her hand on Evie's arm. "Sister," she started solemnly, "is this what you really want?"

Evie sighed. "Yes and no," she said honestly. "I've wanted a job that I can do and enjoy and support myself, but you've all shown me that most everything in life is done with help of one kind or another. So, I've chosen something I think I'll love. It's something I've been considering since...well, since before all the soap fiascos. In that aspect. Yes. This is what I want."

"And no?"

She shot her sisters a watery smile. "Freeman is marrying Helen. There's not one thing I can do about it but wish them the very best in their life together."

She had hoped by saying it out loud it would start to take root. Perhaps in no time at all she would even believe it herself.

Thursday night and once again everyone had gathered at the Bylers' bonus room.

As was expected of him, Freeman had brought Helen to the get-together. However, as *he* expected, she was swept away in a tide of laughing young women who wanted to talk about Helen's adventures and her change of heart in marrying Freeman and staying in Millers Creek.

He could barely allow his gaze to skip around the room for fear that it would slam into Evie's, and the crash would be so loud it would alert everyone around them. After ten or fifteen minutes, he came to realize that she wasn't there. Naomi was there, along with Sarah Ann and Lizzie, but no Evie.

What did he expect? That she would show up chin in the air and congratulate him and Helen? She was strong, but even the strongest women had breaking points. He had pushed Evie to hers.

She'll heal.

The words didn't comfort him any. They were the truth, but he knew the time it would take, the sacrifices that she had made, the times he had pulled her out of the fringes and into the thoroughfare. He felt as if he had been toying with her even though that had never been his intent. He could only hope and pray that after a while, maybe a year or so, she would come to understand and accept why he had done what he did and maybe the three of them could continue on as friends. Yet he knew the dream was like a moonbeam. It could seem as tangible as anything around him, but it would slip through his fingers and be gone in an instant.

At least his decision had pulled Helen out of her deep sadness. She was smiling a bit more now, but the action didn't always reach her deep blue eyes. He supposed it wasn't completely settled. They had yet to talk to the bishop. Helen would still have to go in front of the church and confess her sins. Freeman supposed it was up to Leroy Peachy, the bishop, to decide how to proceed from there. He didn't suppose that Leroy would expect him to lie to the community and say that the child was his, but he had a feeling no matter what announcement was made, there would be those who would believe that he should have stood up next to her to confess his own terrible lapse of morals and judgment.

Then Evie would know the truth. He hadn't been able to tell her that he was doing this for an innocent child. He had broken Evie's heart to protect the blameless. He knew that saying those words wouldn't take away the pain she felt. Those words didn't change anything. He knew he would have to tell her soon. She would start to wonder when the wedding was pushed up to the following month.

After an hour of watching everyone flock around Helen while she pretended to be happy, and another thirty minutes of being slapped on the back in congratulations from guys who most likely talked behind his back when Helen left, trying to decide what he had done wrong to lose the most beautiful woman in their group, Freeman was ready to go home.

He went in search of Helen and amazingly enough found her searching for him.

"Can we leave now?" Helen asked him, her voice a bit breathless as if she had been running.

"*Jah*. Sure," he said, thankful that she was as ready to go home as he was.

The night air was cool enough to provide some relief after the warmth of the bonus room, and Freeman took a deep gulp of it, doing his best to pull the shards of his tattered nerves back into place.

It'll get easier, he told himself, and he wanted to believe that it was true. His *mamm* would tell him the same thing, though he hadn't told his parents the entire truth about his reconciliation with Helen. All things in good time.

Neither one of them said a word as he helped Helen into the buggy, and they started off back toward her house.

"Did you promise Evie that you were going to marry her?" Her question crashed through the night and sliced into his heart.

"No," he said. He hadn't promised her. He hadn't thought he needed to, but he had asked her. Did that make it a promise? Was he splitting hairs to avoid the conversation that was sure to follow?

"But you asked her?"

"It doesn't matter now," he said. He meant it. He had made his choice.

"Really?" Helen turned in place and pinned him, her eyes blazing through the dark. She was angry, but he wasn't sure why. That while she was off in Lancaster, he had taken up with a wonderful woman he'd known practically his entire life?

"Helen—"

"Did you?"

"Jah," he quietly admitted.

"And you're going to break that promise and marry me now."

"You know there's more to it than that."

Helen shook her head. "Do you love her?"

"Where is this coming from?" He flicked his gaze in her direction and then back again to the road ahead of him. He wished she hadn't started such an intense conversation when he was trying to drive on the main roads in the dark.

"Do you love her?"

"Jah." He swallowed hard, the action painful as if he had somehow forgotten how.

"As a wife?"

"Jah." He was going to choke if she kept this up. He hadn't been prepared for this. He had prepped himself to withstand the onslaught from their buddy bunch, but he hadn't expected a barrage of hard-to-answer questions from Helen.

"Do you love me?" The question was so

quiet he could barely hear it over the clop of the horse's hooves and the whir of the wheels on the asphalt.

"I always have." That one was easy enough.

"As a wife?"

He stumbled over his words, his thoughts racing, his heart pounding. He hesitated a moment too long, the small gap of silence more telling than any answer he could give.

"I see."

"Helen…" Thankfully they had reached the side road that led to her house. There was a small turnaround immediately past the stop sign. He pulled the buggy over where he could have the conversation without having to worry about oncoming traffic.

"It's all right, Freeman. I understand."

"Many marriages have been built on less."

She nodded once, then shook her head. "But I can't marry you."

"What?"

"I said—"

"I heard what you said. I'm asking why."

"Because you love another, and I can't come between that." She placed her hands on the sides of his face, cupping his cheeks in her palms. The touch was both strange and familiar. "I love you as a friend. I always will, but if

Evie holds your heart, she's the one you should be marrying."

"The baby—"

"The baby's not your responsibility. It never was. I'm the one who strayed. I'm the one who needs to face the consequences of that action. Not you and Evie both."

He understood what she meant. If he and Helen were to get married, all three of them would pay for Helen's transgressions. Yet that was the exact reason why he had agreed to marry her. It was the right thing to do.

"You're entirely too noble," she said with a small laugh. She turned her face away for a moment, and he could see the tears on her cheeks, dripping off the edge of her jaw. "Go," she finally said. "Drop me off and go by and see Evie. Tell her that you love her and that you're going to keep the promise you made to her when she was just a little girl."

Chapter Sixteen

"Be glad you didn't go," Lizzie said once she came home from the Thursday buddy bunch get-together. She was standing at the dresser in their shared room, looking into the mirror to meet Evie's gaze. "Imogene Peight was there. She brought some sort of buffalo chicken dip that was almost too hot to eat." She took off her prayer *kapp*, removed the pins holding her bob in place, then shook her head. Her long dark brown ponytail trailed down her back. Then she reached for her kerchief to cover her hair. When she turned around, she waved her hand in front of her mouth as if fanning flames.

"What was Imogene doing there?" Evie asked from her place on the bed. She had been sitting up, reading a book and waiting for her sisters to get home. All day she had been out getting her puppies adjusted.

She called them puppies, but they were full-grown dogs. One male, one female, and neither one weighed over five pounds. They were outside in their new kennels that her father had built exclusively for them. Soon Evie would breed them and begin her new puppy business. All in all, it was a satisfying and not tiring day, but for the most part it kept her mind off Freeman. And Helen.

"You know how Imogene is," Sarah Ann said, without a trace of disdain in her voice. She had already changed into her nightgown and was sitting on Lizzie's bed until it was time to go to the room she shared with Priscilla, the twins in their cribs in the room next door. "She keeps a tight rein on Rudy."

"That's one way of putting it," Lizzie said.

Evie nodded. She wasn't sure if Imogene was anxious that something was going to happen to her oldest son or merely controlling. Maybe it was a bit of both.

"Plus, she feels like as the deacon's wife she should chaperone," Sarah Ann said. "That's what Rebecca Yoder said anyway." She snapped her lips together, her expression immediately apologetic. "Oh, Evie, I'm sorry."

"It's okay," Evie replied. "Really. It's not like you're going to have to go your entire life without mentioning him or anyone in his family to me ever again." She was okay now. It had taken a while for her to stop crying. These days it seemed as if she was only a sideways breath away from tears.

She wanted to ask if he was there tonight, but she knew that he was. Of course he was, with Helen.

"I overheard something juicy," Lizzie said, tucking her legs under her so she was kneeling on the bed. "I don't think it's true, though. I mean how can it be true?"

"It might help us decide if you would tell us what it is." Evie gave a small chuckle. See? She would get through this.

"What—what is?" Priscilla asked from the doorway. "The girls are down for the night. Tell me what all I missed." Priscilla was a widow with two small children and didn't feel right about going to the regular youth group meetings, even if she was still young enough. And she was definitely lively enough to want the latest gossip in their group. She perched on the bed next to Lizzie.

"Do tell." Sarah Ann braced her behind on the edge of the dresser, and the sisters waited for one of their own to spill it.

Now that she had all their attention, Lizzie shook her head. "Maybe I shouldn't repeat it. It's really bad if it's true."

"Then definitely tell us," Priscilla said.

Evie managed a small laugh once more. It would take some time, but the dull ache in her chest would ease and she would be able to face the rest of the days of her life without Freeman. Though a small part of her wanted to move in with a cousin in a different church district so she wouldn't have to see Freeman and Helen every other Sunday for the rest of her life or until they had to be realigned.

"I heard…" Lizzie paused. Evie wasn't sure if she was simply being dramatic or if she truly was hesitant to say whatever it was out loud. "It has to do with Freeman." She looked to Evie. "Is that okay?"

Evie shrugged. They had already gone this far.

"Helen is going to have a baby."

Gasps went up all around but none as loud as Evie's own. Could it really be true? She mulled over the prospect as Priscilla and Sarah Ann began questioning Lizzie.

Who said it?

How would they know?

Do you think it's true?

For a moment they seemed to have forgotten all about her. So, she sat quietly and stewed in the idea of it being the truth. It would explain why Helen, who was having the time of her life, decided to suddenly come back to Millers Creek. Why Freeman, who had asked her to marry him, allowing him to fulfill the silly little promise he had made to her twenty years ago, suddenly decided that he needed to marry Helen instead.

She had believed him when he told her that he was in love with Helen. Maybe he was. Maybe that part was the truth. But if there was a baby…

There would be a quick wedding, a small celebration out of season. Not all day eating, visiting and playing wedding games. Quick and done and moving on in the name of forgiveness.

They would have to stand in front of the church and confess their transgressions and ask for forgiveness from the church and from God.

Of course, they would be forgiven and that would be that.

Yes, it really explained a lot.

Except…she didn't see Freeman as the type of man to press a girl into a situation such as that. She surely didn't see Helen succumbing to such a request. If it were true though, then it surely explained a lot.

"Evie?"

She looked up to find her three sisters staring at her. Apparently, they had called her name more than once. *"Jah?"*

"Are you all right?" Priscilla asked.

Sarah Ann sat down next to her on the bed and rubbed her knee through the thin cotton of her nightgown.

"Of course," she said, acting as if it were every day that a person had to wade through such scandalous news.

From outside she could hear the dogs barking, her pair of Yorkies. The female was named Sassy and the male, Butch. It seemed someone had a sense of humor.

Evie had gotten them settled down before she came up to get ready for bed, but something had disturbed them. Or maybe they weren't as settled in as she had believed.

Plink.

"Did you hear that?" Lizzie asked. "That's the third time that noise has sounded."

"The dogs?" Evie asked, wondering if she should go down and see to them or if that would only make tomorrow night worse.

"No, that other sound."

No one spoke for a moment. Then she heard it, in between the barks and howls of the Yorkies.

Plink.

"There it is again." Priscilla went over to the window, opening the shade and looking out into the night. "I'll be."

"You'll be what?" Sarah Ann asked.

Priscilla turned and looked back to Evie. "Freeman is down there."

"In the yard?" Evie asked.

"Jah."

That must be what disturbed Sassy and Butch.

Lizzie joined Priscilla at the window. She unlocked the latch and pushed it up. The *plink* of falling stones could be heard with the motion even over the barks of the tiny dogs. "Apparently throwing rocks at the window."

"Freeman, what are you doing down there?" Priscilla asked in what Evie thought was called a stage whisper. Loud enough that he could hear her over the dogs but not so loud as to wake their *dat* or the babies. All three of whom could be awake already from the noise Sassy and Butch were making to alert them to Freeman being in their yard.

"…Evie…" It was the only word that she could make out.

Lizzie turned, her brows raised in a knowing sort of way. "Sister," she started as if she were delivering news to the world, "Freeman

Yoder is downstairs and wishes for you to join him. What shall I tell him?"

Did she really want to talk to Freeman now, after everything she had just learned?

What if it wasn't true?

She shook her head. "It's late," she said, using the first excuse that came to mind.

"She can't," Lizzie called back.

"Please...important."

Lizzie turned back to Evie. Priscilla spun as well, crossing her arms and waiting for Evie's answer.

"What are you going to do?" Sarah Ann asked.

"I don't know," Evie replied.

"What if he's coming here to tell you the truth about Helen?" Sarah Ann said.

"How would he know we were talking about it?" Priscilla shot back.

"Please..." His voice came to her again.

"Evie?" Lizzie asked.

How could she not go see him? It didn't matter if he went back on his promise, if he didn't want to marry her, even if he got Helen pregnant—they were friends and had been for a long time. If she cut him out of her life for these mistakes, there would be a big gaping hole. A hole no one else would be able to fill.

But tonight, things felt too raw. Still too tender to prod and going downstairs to talk to Freeman would be like pressing on a new bruise.

"She'll be right down," Lizzie called back, not minding her tone the same as Priscilla.

"Shhh," Priscilla admonished. "You'll wake up everyone in the house."

"I don't think I should—" Evie didn't get her sentence finished before Lizzie had hoisted her to her feet.

"Really, I—" she tried to protest.

"You'll need this." Priscilla shoved her arms into a thick dressing gown, and Sarah Ann held out her crutches for her to take.

"I don't—" she tried again, even though she was obviously covered enough to go downstairs. She still wore her kerchief over her hair. Her attire was a little bit on the intimate side, but she was still modest.

"Go quick, before Dat wakes up and finds you outside with Freeman Yoder."

Evie shook her head. "It's not like that."

Whatever it was that he had come to say… well, it more than likely had to do with the rumor spreading around their get-together tonight. He realized that she would be hurt by the knowledge, and he also figured that she would find out from her sisters even though she hadn't attended the meeting herself. It was damage control of a friendship. If their remaining relationship meant enough to him to come here so late at night, then surely it should mean enough to her for her to meet him downstairs.

They walked down the hall together, all four of them, Priscilla stopping at the door to the twins' room to check on them. Miraculously enough they were still sleeping like...well, babies.

Maneuvering the stairs was never something Evie enjoyed, but she climbed them when necessary. Part of that stubborn, independent streak her sisters were always talking to her about. But this was important. There wasn't an empty downstairs bedroom in their *dat*'s house like there was at Mattie's. So down the stairs she went, trying hard not to clank with each step she took. She didn't want to wake their *dat*. He knew she and Freeman were friends, but she didn't know how Thomas Ebersol would take her standing outside in her nightclothes with him at this hour.

Her sisters were right behind her.

"Nuh-uh," she said, shaking her head and pointing back up the stairs with one crutch. "This is private."

They all took two steps back but still followed her despite her fussing all the way to the first floor.

"Evie, can you tell me what's going on down here?"

Dat was up, and he didn't look happy. He was one of those early to bed, early to rise folks, even earlier than most of the Amish farmers they knew. Evie also knew he liked to go to his room and read Westerns when no one was around. He could have been asleep, or he could have been at a very exciting part in his book. It was anyone's guess.

"Freeman's here to see Evie," one of the sisters told off. Evie wasn't sure which one, but she thought it was Lizzie. It was definitely Lizzie's style.

"Is that why your dogs are carrying on?" he asked.

"Probably," Evie said, wishing she had a way to clear through all of this and get outside to find out what Freeman wanted. "It is their first night."

"What is Freeman doing here at this time of night?" her father demanded.

"I'm not sure," Evie said. "That's why I'm down here."

"Send him on his way," her father said. "Quietly. And hush those dogs up before the neighbors call the police." He didn't wait for Evie's acknowledgment before turning on his heel to march back into his room.

Evie looked back at her sisters, all gathered in a cluster of nosiness at the bottom of the staircase. "You three stay here," she said, using her sternest voice. Not that it was all that stern despite her efforts. "Please." So, she would resort to begging.

"Only if you tell us everything," Priscilla bargained.

Evie shook her head and waved one hand, that arm still in the cuff of her crutch. "Fine. But stay put."

To her surprise, her sisters remained in the same spot as Evie let herself out of the house.

The house Thomas Ebersol and his wife, Anna, had chosen to raise their children had a wide porch perfect for visiting. Except that the swing and table with chairs were set right under the large bay window in the living room. She was certain her sisters were now gathered around the window holding their breath so they would catch every word.

Evie eased herself onto the swing as Freeman came around the side of the house.

Once he was out of sight, the pups settled

down, their job done. They had chased off the boogeyman.

"I'msorrythankyouI'msosorryIjusthadto—" He was practically out of breath as he collapsed down in the chair closest to where she sat.

"What's wrong, Freeman?" She braced herself for the truth, glad for once that Imogene Peight was spreading rumors. At least she would be ready for this one.

"Nothing," Freeman said, sucking in a breath and obviously trying to get control of himself once again. "Everything. Nothing."

"Which is it?" Evie asked, still braced for the worst. The *everything* part.

"Where did the dogs come from?" He wanted to talk about that now?

"I'm going to breed them and sell the puppies."

"Puppies," he said, mulling it over like it was a new concept he had never heard of. "I can get behind that."

"Get behind—" She stopped as he reached over and took up her hand from where it lay in her lap.

"Evie Ebersol, will you marry me?"

Evie tugged her hand free and stared at him, her brow wrinkling in confusion. "Marry you?" She pushed to her feet, clumsily snatching up her crutches to go back into the house. "Is this some kind of joke, Freeman Yoder?"

"No," he said, quietly standing and blocking her path. "Please, Evie, hear me out."

She had already heard enough tonight, enough crazy, heartbreaking rumors. She wasn't sure she was ready for the devastating truth.

"You can't marry me," she finally said, though she stopped trying to get away from him. He was bigger and stronger and more agile, but the truth was she wanted to be close to him even if only for a little bit tonight. She had missed him. Terribly. "You're going to marry Helen." Exactly the way it had always been.

He shook his head. "I'm not marrying Helen."

Then perhaps she wasn't going to have a baby, and the rumor was just that, a rumor.

"Sit down and listen to me, please."

She returned to her seat on the swing, and he sat back on the chair next to it. The one where he could reach out and grab her hand. She knew she shouldn't have, but she let him. Even if only to feel close to him on this night. Perhaps the last night. Yet if what he was saying was true…

"I'm not marrying Helen," he said again. "I want to marry you."

"I don't understand," she finally said. "You came to me days ago telling me that you loved her and wanted to be with her."

"I was trying to do the right thing. Turns out it wasn't right after all."

"Perhaps you should start at the beginning."

He did, telling her all about Helen's return, the child she carried and how he only wanted to help his friend in need and the baby she would one day give birth to.

"What changed your mind?" Evie asked.

He smiled. "Helen did. She said she didn't want to stand in the way of true love and a twenty-year-old promise."

Evie narrowed her eyes at him. "Not that again," she said, but the weight had lifted from her heart. She still wasn't sure what Helen was going to do. Most likely go away and have the baby only to let it be adopted by a couple who couldn't have their own children. Maybe even her sister Hannah and Hannah's husband, Reuben.

"A promise is a promise," he said again. Evie felt sure that he believed if he said it enough times that she would eventually begin to believe him. Maybe…

"You promised Helen that you would help her," Evie reminded him. She had to clear ev-

erything out of the way before she could let her
heart have free rein to hope.

"I promised you first."

She shook her head. "That's silly."

"What if I told you that Helen wants her true
love as well?"

Evie didn't know what to say to that. Helen's
true love had always been Freeman, with Evie
always off to one side.

"I'm not going to lie and say that she'll have
it easy, but Helen wants to face this situation
she has found herself in in the most honorable
fashion she can."

Her heart went out to her friend. Why hadn't
she told Evie about the baby? She supposed that
would be a hard secret to share. Even with a
best friend.

"This is honorable? Me and you getting married? Helen going off or whatever?"

"Helen's going to be fine," he said, his confidence inspiring. "The Lord will see to her."

The Lord would take care of them all.

"And that leaves us with true love," he said.
"Me and you. And the puppies."

True love. Could it be that simple?

He tilted his head to one side and studied
her. "Are you going to be this stubborn after
we're married?"

Her heart once again jumped at the thought of being married to Freeman. The only man she had ever loved.

"It's not necessary," he continued. "You can allow yourself to be happy."

Was that what she was doing?

"You don't have to put everyone else's happiness before your own."

"I'm not sure I know how to do that," she admitted.

"It's okay." He smiled at her, and she knew that everything was going to be fine. "I'll help you. With the two of us working together, you will have your happy ending."

"I will?" she whispered, wanting to believe.

He leaned forward in his seat and lightly touched his lips to hers in the merest hint of a kiss. "Guaranteed."

* * * * *

*Be sure to look for the next book
by Amy Lillard, available October 2025
wherever Love Inspired novels are sold!*

Dear Reader,

Welcome back to Millers Creek, Pennsylvania, nestled in the lovely Kishacoquillas Valley. The first time I ever visited Kish Valley, I was blown away by its beauty. Patchwork fields checkered over rolling foothills, two mountains practically side by side and a winding two-lane road through the middle of it all. It was a postcard come to life.

After that first trip, I knew I wanted to set a story there, and Millers Creek was born. Since then, I have traveled that road many times, looking for yellow buggies, phone shanties and one-room schoolhouses—just some of the most charming aspects of life in the valley.

To me the most interesting part of the Amish culture is not all the traits they share, but their own diversity. So alike and yet so different. From each other and from us *Englischers*. It's what keeps me coming back to write books about these intriguing people who go at life at a slower pace and yet somehow are side by side with us all.

If you would like to learn more about my Amish travels and books, check out my website

dedicated to just that: amysamishadventures.
com. Be sure to let me know you stopped by.
I love hearing from readers.

Thanks, blessings and all my best,
Amy